"Truly," he said of his that wou around inside l of beauty, Chloe.

"So are you, Lao," she said softly, then found herself smiling when he looked surprised she should compliment him in return.

It made her wonder if he was so overwhelming, so wildly intense, and so astronomically remote in every way that mattered, that no one bothered to offer him compliments. But any such thoughts splintered, because he carried her hand to his lips and pressed a courtly sort of kiss to her knuckles.

It should have felt silly and old-fashioned, but it didn't. Not in an ancient castle, perched here above an island so steeped in history.

And not when the faint brush of his lips across the back of her hand made everything inside her seem to curl up tight, then begin to boil.

"Welcome, little one," he murmured, the heat in his gaze making everything inside her take notice, especially the tender flesh between her legs. And that heart of hers that would not stop its wild thundering. "To our wedding night. At last."

USA TODAY bestselling, RITA® Award-nominated and critically acclaimed author **Caitlin Crews** has written more than a hundred and thirty books and counting. She has a masters and PhD in English literature, thinks everyone should read more category romance and is always available to discuss her beloved alpha heroes—just ask. She lives in the Pacific Northwest with her comic book–artist husband, is always planning her next trip and will never, ever read all the books in her to-be-read pile. Thank goodness.

Books by Caitlin Crews

Harlequin Presents

Willed to Wed Him
A Secret Heir to Secure His Throne

The Outrageous Accardi Brothers

The Christmas He Claimed the Secretary
The Accidental Accardi Heir

Pregnant Princesses

The Scandal That Made Her His Queen

The Lost Princess Scandal

Crowning His Lost Princess
Reclaiming His Ruined Princess

Visit the Author Profile page
at Harlequin.com for more titles.

Caitlin Crews

WHAT HER SICILIAN HUSBAND DESIRES

ISBN-13: 978-1-335-73937-7

What Her Sicilian Husband Desires

Copyright © 2023 by Caitlin Crews

Harlequin Enterprises ULC
22 Adelaide St. West, 41st Floor
Toronto, Ontario M5H 4E3, Canada
www.Harlequin.com

Printed in U.S.A.

WHAT HER SICILIAN HUSBAND DESIRES

CHAPTER ONE

It was a beautiful day for a divorce.

Chloe Stapleton smiled to herself as the private jet winged its way down over the mountains of Sicily that rose up from the gleaming Mediterranean Sea, jutting proudly high and covered in sprawling vineyards and crumbling old temples to honor gods long lost.

That felt appropriate too.

She kept her gaze trained out through the window as the plane came in for a brisk landing on a remote hilltop strip, carved into the mountains with a certain brutal efficiency that reminded her of the owner of not only the plane, but the landing strip too. And the whole bloody mountain, the better part of Sicily, not to mention an ever-widening swath of the whole wide world beyond.

For there was no part of the planet, however isolated and far away, that the might and power of the Monteleone family did not reach.

Chloe was already feeling a bit nostalgic that she was very shortly going to be asked to resign from her place as one of them.

Or rather, one of them in name only, she amended.

She had been to this estate only once before. Five years ago, when she hadn't known what to do, so she'd reached out to the darkly powerful man who had once been her stepbrother to beg him for help.

He had been her only hope—and Lao Monteleone had not hesitated. She always thought of him as a smooth coil of a man, forever holding himself back from the unwary—which only made his ruthless ferocity all the more apparent. When she knew, as did the world, that he did exactly what suited him when and how he liked.

But he had always been kind to her, if distant.

She had come all the way here five years ago, banking on that kindness, and Lao had not let her down.

As she stepped out of the plane and allowed his always excruciatingly well-trained staff to usher her into the waiting car, she could admit that Lao's kindness—and the protection he had offered her immediately—had made her feel safe when she hadn't believed she would ever feel such a thing again. She would never forget that.

In the darkest hour of her grief, when she had

lost her father and with him, the one person who had always loved her and championed her in all things, Lao had stepped in. He had taken care of everything, allowing Chloe to take care of herself.

It was truly bittersweet to return here today, knowing full well that this must be the end of that safety. That she would need to find a way to be her own safe space from here on out.

Surely this is simply called learning to be an adult, Chloe told herself stoutly. *Get a hold of yourself, girl.*

She tried to brush the strange melancholy away as the car took her down from the landing strip on narrow track roads that wound around the exuberantly wild mountains, giving her sweeping views of the ancient Sicilian cities down near the water and the many historic villages tucked into the hills. Back home in London, the weather was predictably vile, making the sunshine appear even more bountiful here. It seemed like a blessing, pouring down through the trees and making the leaves gleam brightly as she drove through.

Even five years ago, when she had still felt so inside out in the face of her father's loss, it had been impossible not to notice the beauty of this untamed island. While she had spent many holidays in the more refined parts of Italy before then—the hills of Tuscany, the canals of Venice, the beaches

of the Amalfi Coast—she had never come to Sicily
before or since. And it made that nostalgia within
her seem to ache all on its own to find it just as
she remembered it. A wild tangle, not quite civilized, and in no way as manicured as the Italy
thought she knew.

But then, the same could be said for Lao himself.

He had married her here five years ago, quickly
and without ceremony. It had been more like a
business meeting than a wedding, she thought,
though at the time it had pleased her, for it was a
demonstration of his kindness. They'd stood together in Lao's office, here on this mysterious island in the ancient castle he had renovated and
made the base of his operations.

The castle, he had informed her offhandedly
five years ago, that had been in the Monteleone
family for some untold number of centuries. That
had made their marriage seem even more like a
safe haven, she'd thought then. As if all of those
centuries, steeped in Monteleone might and power
and influence, would cocoon her, too.

She supposed it had.

When Chloe thought back to that day, it was
all tearstained and blurry. She had the impression
of Lao's steel gray eyes and his powerful form,
so much broader and taller than she was. As if he

intended to block out the sky if that was what she wished. And the way he held her pale hands in his, belting out the appropriate words.

"A marriage such as this, naturally, will be in name only," he had told her in that powerfully grim way of his.

"Naturally," she had murmured in reply.

And it was between her and the dreams she'd never shared with another living soul that she might have found that *just* the slightest bit insulting. That there had been a part of her, even then, even so lost in the terrible clenching fist of that grief had not left her for another year or so, that had been…not exactly *insulted* that Lao had not even bothered to seal their marriage with a kiss. That he had glared at the priest as if even requesting such a thing was an affront.

She hadn't been *insulted*, of course she hadn't in the face of his going so far above and beyond any possible duty he might have felt, but she had felt ever so slightly *indignant* all the same.

But that was pure silliness and well did she know it.

What mattered, as she intended to make certain she told Lao when she saw him, was that it was a gift. All of it, when he'd owed her nothing. When he could so easily have refused to even see her that day. He had given her the gift of his protection, and her silly, foolish little fantasies were a secret she would take with her to her grave.

The car turned in through an imposing gate, flanked by ancient bits of marble, though the gate itself was decidedly modern and clearly high-tech. Once through that gate, the dirt track became smoother, so there was less jolting and jumping, and she no longer needed to grip the handle in the back seat so tightly.

Chloe settled in as the car headed up the drive toward the man—the *husband*, mad word though it was to describe either Lao or his relationship to her—waiting for her. Cypress trees marched in dutiful columns on either side of the lane, olive trees were set into neat lines down the flank of a rolling hill, and she could catch glimpses of the cultivated Monteleone land in all directions. But it was the old castle that made her hold her breath when she caught sight of it, rising in its ancient, imposing way there at the top of Lao's own, private mountain.

The place where he had taken the sobbing mess she'd been, married her, then set her free to do as she liked.

"As your father would have wished," he had told her, almost formerly, in the brief moments they'd stood together after the quick ceremony.

And so Chloe had spent these years that Lao

had gifted her doing her best to find her own place in the world because that, she knew, was what her father would have wanted for her if it had been up to him. If he'd been here to listen to her stories and laugh away her hurts until they felt minor.

But the truth was that she'd always been a bit too dreamy. Maybe a better word was *sheltered*, but either way, she'd drifted from one job to another, forever trying to find her *passion*. She'd done a bit of literary PR, because it had sounded so grand to swan about London, talking of books to whoever would listen. But the job hadn't worked out that way. It was much less about talking, very little about loving books at all, and a whole lot more about tracking campaigns across the internet and avoiding angry emails from authors. She'd dipped in and out the charities and nonprofits that a great many of her school friends were involved in. But they all seemed to be more about being photographed at parties than actually doing any good in the world. None of her friends had understood when she tried to tell them how she felt.

"It does good in the world," her best friend Mirabelle had argued with a roll of her lacquered eyes. "People like to look at pretty things, Chloe. Why not be one of them?"

Chloe had eventually ended up working in an art gallery, which she found fun. Because the gallery was filled mostly by the sorts of people who enjoyed making the most spectacular mountains out of any given molehill.

"That's how you convince a rich man with no taste to buy a splatter of paint on a crap canvas to bung up on the guest room wall," her jaded boss, the sleek and slinky Moriah, had told her.

Maybe, Chloe had started to think, she was onto something with the art world. Because, at the very least, she wasn't as bored as she'd been in publicity. Surely that was worth *something*. Maybe it wasn't *her passion*, but then, maybe it was deeply unsophisticated to spend so much time worrying about finding something no one else seemed to care about or value at all.

Maybe she needed to worry more about upping her sophistication game, she'd been thinking in the days before she'd received Lao's summons.

Strange, then, that the only thing she could seem to think about as the car wound ever closer to Castello Monteleone was passion, after a fashion. She was already working on her arguments. The same way she did every time she received a summons from Lao in whatever city they both happened to be in, because he always knew where she was. Once, memorably, she'd met up with him on a beach in Brazil. He usually took her for a meal, quizzed her on her life and plans as if he was taking over the role of her father and guardian despite being her legal husband, and then left her reeling in the wake of all of that rampant virility, and seething, incalculable power.

She always had the dreams after those dinners.

But this was the first summons she'd received to the castle in all this time. Chloe had known the minute she'd received it that it could only mean one thing.

The one thing she'd known would come, sooner or later.

Lao had given her the gift of these five years, held securely there between his might and influence.

It was high time she stood on her own two feet, however unsophisticated. She knew that.

But knowing it didn't make those feet seem any more steady or sophisticated when the car pulled up to the castle's grand entrance, and his staff swung the door open to wave her out.

She was dearly tempted to crumple into a swoon like one of her favorite heroines from a book, but she didn't.

Because that would be taking advantage. And would cheapen, somehow, the care Lao had taken of the truly beset girl who had shown up here in pieces the last time, uninvited and wholly uncertain if she'd make it through the week.

She made herself smile at the poker-faced servant who held the car door for her, and again at the extensively trained butler who bowed her into the castle's great hall before personally leading her deep within.

Chloe wasn't much for architecture, and she hadn't paid much attention to her surroundings five years ago, but she could see now that this place was a true wonder. No doubt it helped to have all the money in the world, but she thought that Lao must have a particularly keen eye for detail as well. Because he had taken this ancient castle and made it a showpiece of timeless style and incomparable grace. There were stone walls all around, complete with ancient hung tapestries and priceless art in museum-quality frames. At the same time, there were also boldly modern steel girders and the feeling of brightness, airiness, and more windows than there could possibly have been originally. She had read once, after visiting this place the first time, that he had essentially taken a ruin that had stood on the property for generations— instead of the family villa that was stationed somewhere else on the land—and transformed it into his own personal palace.

A feat of architectural time travel, the article writer had gushed. *A heady, dizzying example of taste and vision, refinement taken to perfection.*

Yet when she thought of those words, she pictured Lao himself, not the castle that loomed all around her now.

The butler led her over the glassed-in bridge that spanned a deep crevice winnowed into the side of the mountain, allowing her to gaze down for what seemed like miles. She felt a shiver start deep within her, winding around and around with every step until it took her over. She could feel the goose bumps all over her skin. And when they reached the other side and found themselves in another hall, she could *see* the way her skin bristled as they walked along what seemed like an entire wall of antique mirrors. Chloe took the opportunity to smooth down her hair and straighten the clothes she'd worn on the flight down from London this morning.

She'd dressed for her imposing husband, despite the fact that he was soon to be her ex.

Because no matter what he was to her, he had always rendered her a bit breathless. Whether he was wearing a dark bespoke suit in the grim rain of a London summer or lounging beachside in Brazil with an indolence she hadn't been able to look at directly.

Or maybe it was less the indolence that had been so blinding and more the acres upon acres of lean, golden muscles that had been on display, with the dusting of dark black hair, and that entrancing V etched into his lower abdomen that led the eye directly to one of those astonishingly small bathing costumes stretched to capacity over his—

But thinking of that meeting in Brazil made her cheeks burn. She couldn't recall a single word he'd said. It was possible she hadn't spoken at all, but had merely been sat there in a tumultuous daze.

Thinking only of the color blue.

The color of that bathing costume.

It haunted her still.

And again, Chloe found herself smiling at her own silliness as the butler murmured something she didn't quite catch, then beckoned for her to precede him into the room she remembered so well.

She had been married here, on this edge-of-the-cliff office that could only be called such a thing because there was a desk on one end, surrounded by crisp white bookshelves, all of them filled—but not bursting. Every item on every shelf was precisely placed *just so*. But then, everything in this part of the castle was new, from the poured concrete floor tossed here and there with rich, deeply hued artisanal rugs, and the grand wall of windows that aped the castle next door, but were all in glass.

It was there, standing before that glass that she knew gave way to the cliff side itself, that she saw him.

Right there where she had married him five years ago.

Lao Monteleone himself, standing with his back to her.

Chloe wondered if it was possible to be jet-lagged when she had only flown a few hours down to Sicily from England. Because she couldn't think of any other reason why she suddenly felt so weak.

He turned, then, and the sunlight poured in from above, illuminating the harsh planes of his stern face. And then she found she wasn't simply weak. She wasn't even breathless, as usual. She was holding her breath. Completely.

Because it was always like this, and yet always seemed new. Lao was a hard, shocking blow to her solar plexus every time she saw him. As if she'd fallen down and had the breath knocked straight out of her.

He was widely called handsome, though he wasn't. He was too imposing. Too forbidding. Taken apart, his features were too strong for the kind of male beauty that most admired and therefore graced magazine covers and the like. Those high cheekbones, that ruthless blade of a nose. Starkly sensual lips that were forever pressed in a faintly disapproving line, as now.

He was imposing, though she knew by now that was as much the power that emanated from him as his actual skeletal structure. He was at least six feet and muscled, everywhere, like so many of the statues in the halls of this castle. But his shoulders were wider than anything carved in the Renaissance or since.

Today, he was not dressed in his usual bespoke suit or, mercifully, a thong bathing costume in cobalt blue, though Chloe would not describe him as *casual*, either. Even lounging mostly naked, gleaming in the Brazilian sun, he had exuded all the might and formality that he always did.

At least today there was no need to swallow her tongue.

Even if she could see a hint of his sun-gold skin at the top of that crisp white button-down shirt he wore.

She had no idea why merely *looking* at him should make a raw swath of a nearly unbearable ache widen within her.

Only that she was certain he could see it. Just as she was sure that he could see the bright spots of heat still on her cheeks.

"Hello, Lao," she said, and felt the absurd urge she always did, to break out into giggles like a schoolgirl. She felt that fluttery thing inside her take over, filling up that aching part until it was hard to tell where one bit began and the other ended.

Looking at him felt the same as peering down

into the jagged Sicilian canyons that could easily eat her whole.

"Chloe." Her name on his lips was the same dark poetry it always was, inflected with the magic of his accent, like so much spice. It was a chore not to lick her lips. "I trust your flight was pleasant?"

"Yes, thank you. Very pleasant indeed."

"I have ordered you some tea," he said, and she did not miss the emphasis on that last word.

Lao was entirely Italian. He did not understand the English obsession with tea, much less diluted with milk. But was providing it anyway, because that was what he did, she knew. He took care of things, always. It made a different sort of shiver work its way through her that she, alone in all the world, should know this man for the protector he truly was. Not the dark mage of the business world that so many feared, the inscrutable billionaire who had been, at times, the most hated man in Europe. She alone knew better.

His gray eyes flared with a touch of silver heat. "I know how you English rely upon your tea."

"That sounds lovely." Chloe would have said it was lovely even if it wasn't, but the truth was, she could do with a bracing brew to get her head on straight. She needed to stop shivering and aching and start remembering that this trip was supposed to be about gratitude. About thanks and divorce.

Not cobalt-blue bathing costumes or that chiseled face of his.

Lao nodded to someone behind her, so she turned her head to see the same butler directing another diffident staff member to set up a full tea service on a polished wood table that looked as if it had been hand carved. Perhaps from the trees on this very mountain.

The silence in the room seemed to grow, then deepen, after his staff retreated yet again.

"You're very kind," Chloe said, because she'd promised herself she wouldn't let this get away from her. That she wouldn't let her overwhelming foolishness where this man was concerned leave her tongue tied the way it often did. "I want you to know that I appreciate it more than I could possibly express. These past five years have been a wonderful gift. I don't know what would have become of me without you. It's thanks to you that I feel ready and capable to carry on now. On my own. But I'll always remember this, Lao. It was a truly wonderful thing for you to do for me, when technically, you weren't even my stepbrother anymore."

He didn't move, so Chloe wasn't certain why it was that he seemed to *expand* then, taking over the whole world. Certainly this room, though the arched glass ceiling that must have been three stories high at least.

His gaze was a thundercloud. "Why do you think I've called you here today, Chloe?"

"Oh." She laughed nervously, though she wasn't sure why she was laughing at all, or even why she felt so nervous in the first place. This was *Lao*. Sure, he was big and imposing and overwhelming, but he had never been anything but perfectly kind to her. Sweet, even. Her reaction was the *height* of exactly the kind of foolishness that had led to Mirabelle calling her a *right dozy cow* more than once. Mostly affectionately. "Well. I assume that you're ready to go on with the rest of your life. And that an inconvenient marriage to the daughter of a man I don't recall you liked all that much anyway might get in the way of that."

But he only gazed at her, in that same stormy fashion and she found herself too hot, again.

"I'm perfectly happy for you to divorce me, Lao," she said hurriedly. "Really. You don't have to worry about me at all."

"I do not worry about you, because I know you are taken care of," he told her, in a low, stern tone that did nothing at all to take away that shivering inside her. "But things must change, Chloe. Because I think it is high time. Past time, even."

"Past time," she agreed, and once again, lectured herself not to feel that unreasonable sense of disappointment. "I agree."

"I need an heir," he told her, and she had the strangest sense that he was being gentle, though there was nothing about his demeanor that would suggest he was capable of it. "And as I already have a wife, I see no reason why she can't provide me with one."

"An heir?" Chloe was having trouble keeping up. She swallowed, though her throat didn't seem to work and her body seemed to have taken itself off for some kind of riot. "Do you...do you mean with me?"

He looked as if he'd made from thunder and too much rain, as wild and untamed as the Sicilian mountain they stood upon. He looked *at her* as if she was a very small, glass thing he held in the palm of his hand.

She felt as if she was.

"I mean you, Chloe," Lao said, like he was rendering judgment. Though she was glass straight through and could only seem to concentrate on that brooding heat of his from across the room. "It is time you became my wife in full."

CHAPTER TWO

LAO MONTELEONE HAD waited what seemed like an unbearable lifetime or three for this moment.

Now it was upon him, it did not disappoint.

He had wanted Chloe Stapleton for a long, long while.

And Lao did not have much experience with *wanting*. What he wanted, he got, and long before he had spent so much as an instant in the *wanting* of it. He had chosen to view his obsession with Chloe Stapleton, perhaps the only thing he could remember waiting for in his entire life, as a lesson. One he had been pleased to learn.

Because it reminded him that he was something more than the current master of the vast Monteleone enterprise. The lord of all he surveyed, etcetera.

It reminded him that he was, beneath all of that, mere flesh and blood and mortal.

A man like any other where it counted most.

Not that he required these reminders today. Because Chloe stood before him the way she always did, with those dreamy, impractical dark chocolate eyes and soft lips that seemed forever on the verge of an exclamation. He knew that she usually dressed far more casually, just as he knew that she like to make an effort when she saw him. He approved, because it meant that she wore a dress like today's that highlighted the delicacy of her clavicle, the soft, elegant sweep of her neck.

All of that was as expected, and he enjoyed it.

But he enjoyed even more the way she looked at him now, a new gleaming thing in her gaze.

Did she even know she wanted him or would he need to teach her that, too?

Lao was more than ready to find out.

"I don't understand," she said, when he rather thought she did.

He crossed the room, not quite brushing past her to take a seat near the tea service that his staff had laid out. He was too Italian to fully understand the lure of endless cups of a milky liquid that was not coffee, and moreover, not confined to breakfast. But that did not prevent him from pouring out the tea, then taking his own cup—mercifully black—and watching as she drifted over to the chair opposite him, as if pulled by some kind of invisible thread.

The way she always did. He approved of that, too.

"I've always expected you to divorce me," she said as she sat, frowning at her teacup. She added the expected milk, then three sugars, and did not seem to note the arch of his brow as she took a big sip. "I assumed that was the plan. We both know that you only married me as a favor. No one on earth would expect you to continue doing me that favor for life."

"I do not wish to divorce you."

"Oh, but you have to." She looked up then, her gaze solemn. And direct, which always came as such a surprise when she wafted about otherwise. "If you want an heir, Lao. It's the only thing that makes sense."

"Not the only thing."

Her lips parted, and she blinked, confusion all over her pretty face. "I'm really not following you. All you have to do is announce that you're looking for a woman to have your baby, and the parade will form within the hour. A parade that could go on for days and days, across several continents."

"I have no need of parades. I am already married. And as I require that my heir be legitimate, this seems an easy solution, do you not think?"

"You're not making sense."

She frowned at him, the first hint he'd seen in some time that there was more to her than the hapless, lost girl she'd become after weathering a year of deaths. First his mother, the complicated and resplendent Portia, who he knew Chloe had adored. As had everyone who had encountered her. Six months later, her father, the brash, self-made Charlie Stapleton—who had lured Portia away from her Monteleone widowhood—followed, leaving Chloe devastated.

Lao had been something less than pleased at his mother's second marriage, a mere eighteen months after his own father's death. That his parents had never been happy together was neither here nor there, to his way of thinking. What did happiness have to do with the Monteleones?

"There is more to life than the Monteleones, Lao," Portia had said on the night she'd confessed to him that she was remarrying. There had been a great wisdom in her gaze, but he had not wished to see it. "Even for you."

He had not allowed her to see anything but the faint pulse of the muscle in his jaw.

"I have seen no evidence to suggest anything of the sort," he had replied.

And he had been surprised—not to mention outraged—that his mother had gone ahead and married Charlie Stapleton anyway. He and the man he had never referred to as his stepfather had never been close. They had suffered through the odd family event, but with precious little grace on both sides.

What Lao remembered most about his mother's wedding was Charlie Stapleton's little girl. She had been cross. And about as interested in their parents' marriage as he had been.

"I expect you are looking forward to having a new mother," he had said to the glowering seven-year-old who had, for reasons unclear to him, been left alone in his presence. He couldn't remember why. Was it the actual wedding, or some attempt at a family meeting before that? He couldn't pull those details into place, but he remembered Chloe. Her arms crossed, her mouth turned down, her hair in dark plaits.

"I already have a mother," the little girl had replied tartly. "She's disappointing. Why would I want another?"

Lao had laughed despite himself, when he'd been so certain that he would never so much as crack a smile while participating in such a farce. He would support his mother, as ever, but he'd had no intention of warming in the slightest to Charlie Stapleton, his new money, or the child he'd had from his scandalous tabloid marriage to an "actress" whose beauty far outstripped her talent.

But he had liked Chloe, was the thing. Despite himself, he'd always liked her. And he'd come to have a grudging respect for Charlie, too, because whatever his many sins, he had loved Lao's mother. In a way his own father not only hadn't, but—Lao was all too aware—had never wanted or attempted.

Monteleones were not emotional. So his father had always taught him. Emotions were for smaller men, who had less consequence and more time to indulge such foolishness. Monteleones had empires upon empires to keep running so smoothly that they were nearly invisible, unless someone knew precisely where to look.

"Real power is never showy," his father had always told him. "That is a performance. Real power does not require a stage."

But Chloe was not a Monteleone. Not back then.

And he had found he liked the funny little girl who was always rattling around the great mansions they found themselves in, her eyes full of dreams and her arms usually piled high with books. She had always amused him, when Lao was not easily amused.

He had not seen her in some while when, not long after her eighteenth birthday, her father had died and she had come all the way to Sicily to seek his aid.

Lao would have given it to her without question, in honor of that funny kid he remembered.

The only child he ever had any interaction with. And because it would have pleased his mother to imagine he might do something, not because of what he might gain from it or how it might enhance his standing or portfolio, but simply because it was the right thing to do.

Portia had been married to Lao's father, a sheer icicle of a man, for years. Yet had still maintained her warmth. She had been a marvel of a woman indeed.

He would have helped Chloe no matter what.

But she'd been standing right here in this room. She had been waiting for him. And she had turned to look at him when he came in.

That was all. Even now, he couldn't have said what it was that had changed everything for him. It had been raining outside, so there had been no convenient shaft of light to illuminate her features. He thought—and he had gone over it so many times in his head by now, again and again and again— that perhaps it was her grief, carving the woman she was becoming indelibly across the features he had only ever seen as that of a girl.

One way or another, a bolt of sheer lust had struck him, so hard he was still shocked it hadn't taken him to the ground. It was as if he had never laid eyes on a woman before, and he had not known whether to be shocked that he was capable of feeling something so intensely—or shocked far more that she had caused it. *Chloe Stapleton*, of all the women alive.

He had assumed he was ill.

Even so, he had handled everything, from summoning a priest to "donating" the appropriate funds to hasten along what was normally a more drawn-out wedding process, here in Italy. Then he married her, sent her on her way, sent a security detail to England to keep eyes on her—on the off chance anyone discovered she was the wife of *the* Lao Monteleone and imagined they could get to him through her—and got back to work.

He had been certain that the strange longing he had felt for Chloe would pass like any other virus, but it did not.

Every now and again, he had met up with his putative wife to see how she was faring, and that bizarre reaction to her had only gotten worse each time. Until he had been forced to face it head-on— after seeing her in a filmy sort of beach cover-up in Brazil that had only drawn attention to what she wore beneath it. And worse, that body of hers that had haunted him ever since.

Golden curves held tight in a blazing red bikini.

Everything since then had been a waiting game, bringing them here. To this moment. To this day, at last.

The day he had finally had enough.

If he must be plagued with this *longing*, he had decided, he might as well use it for a purpose.

Chloe was frowning thoughtfully. She took another sip of her tea. "I didn't think about the fact that, of course, people can make all the babies they like in a doctor's office these days."

Lao could have a disabused her of whatever notion she was having, but he did not. He found himself too intrigued by her, given that he had no idea where she was going when she spoke. Notably unlike everyone else in his orbit. His many underlings did not dare enter his presence unless they were fully vetted and his phalanx of assistants had ascertained exactly how they planned to waste his time.

If any one of them had ever surprised him, Lao could not recall it.

But Chloe was nothing like the people who worked for him, obsequious and sharp at once. He watched instead as some other thought occurred to her. He could see it break across her face, like a tide.

She leaned forward and set her tea down on the table between them, with a decisive sound that was unlike her. "I would love to have a baby for you, Lao. It's a bit extreme, I suppose, but I can't express how much your protection has meant to me all these years. Really, I'd be happy to be a surrogate for you."

"You will not be my surrogate." She frowned at him then, but he remained where he was, sitting untroubled in his chair. "I told you, Chloe. I want a wife. By which I mean, in every way."

That sat there between them, as much a presence as the tea things. The wall of windows. The whole of Sicily just there, outside.

Chloe seemed to freeze solid, and Lao use the opportunity to flip back through all the security reports on her that he had committed to memory, these last five years. He had expected that she would carry on as most eighteen-year-olds in her position—rich and pretty—would have. And it wasn't as if she'd locked herself away in a tower. Quite the opposite. She had attended all the same parties her friends had, but when they'd hopped into taxis with inappropriate men, Chloe had gone home.

He had begun to suspect—then begun to hope—that she was as innocent as she seemed.

It wasn't a requirement. But it was fast becoming an obsession.

Lao told himself it was the novelty, that was all, for a man whose lovers had always been women of great experience and even greater enthusiasm for the things he—and his vast wealth—could do for them.

But this was Chloe. His wife.

"Not every way," she argued.

He only waited.

Because she might be dreamy, and her father might have been so doting that he'd allowed her to grow up in a cruel world this naive, but Lao was neither of those things. His father had raised him the same way that he had been raised in his time. As harshly as possible, to prepare Lao for the enormous task before him. The Monteleone fortune was an entity so broad and so vast it was as if it lived and breathed on its own. It was nearly sentient, this many centuries along. One did not manage it so much as tame it, throughout the course of a lifetime that must necessarily be dedicated entirely to that taming.

Lao had always taken his role seriously. He had not, like so many of the heirs he knew to this kingdom or that fortune, wasted away his youth in the pursuit of foolish things. He had never been tabloid fodder. He was not given to flashiness of any variety. He made certain he did not frequent the kinds of places paparazzi might linger and he avoided the sort of people who trailed cameras and commentary in their wakes.

The Monteleone family had always preferred

their power to rest behind thrones rather than upon them, because that way it could not matter if the regime changed, the way regimes always did with tedious regularity.

The Monteleones remained.

Yet that wasn't to say that Lao had not satisfied each and every one of his appetites in a way that he saw fit. He had, and did. It was only that he preferred that the things he got up to remained his own business and no one else's.

And he was certainly capable of recognizing a deep, hungry feminine interest when he saw it.

He'd been seeing it in Chloe Stapleton for quite some time.

He had not been certain it was real—until Brazil. And he certainly saw it now.

Lucky for her, he was finally ready to do something about it.

Her mouth worked a time or two, though no sound came forth. Her throat moved, and Lao saw goose bumps march up and down her bare arms.

"I think," she said slowly—very slowly, with a look in her dark eyes he could not call the least bit dreamy, "that I need you to tell me exactly what you mean by that."

"I think you know."

She studied him as if the glass walls had shattered and a dragon or two had flown in. As if he *was* a dragon himself. He did not find the idea the least bit outrageous. And he could admit that he did not mind the hint of awe in her dark gaze.

"You can't possibly mean you want *me* to be the sort of wife you want in *every* way," she said at last, her voice more thready than usual.

"I am unaware that I am married to anybody else," he said. He held the delicate teacup in his hand, and kept his voice bland. Though he knew the way he looked at her was nothing of the sort.

She flushed, as if he had his hands on her. "Lao. You can't mean that. You don't. I don't understand what you're going on about, because it can't be…"

But she trailed off, her lips parting as if she could taste the tension in the room, then. At last.

He sipped at his tea, hardly tasting the bitter brew of water over leaves the English liked so well. When all he could see was the way she swayed, slightly, as if whatever images she had in her head were making her shiver where she sat.

It made him conjure up his own.

"What that means, Chloe, is that I want you in my bed," he told her in a low voice, watching with a hard sort of pleasure as her skin pinkened with every word. "Every night. And if it takes some time, all the better. I do not wish to rest the whole of the Monteleone legacy on one head as my parents did. I am thinking four, at the least."

"Children?" she asked, faintly. "You want *four* children?"

"I do," he assured her. And then made certain she understood him fully. "With you, Chloe. I want to have four children with you, the old-fashioned way. Not in a doctor's office. In a bed. Against the wall. Anywhere and everywhere. Is that exact enough for you?"

Lao watched her take that in.

He found himself braced, as if she might take flight. And he did not know that he wished to acknowledge the part of him that wanted her to do exactly that, so that he might have the pleasure of chasing her.

Like the kind of barbarian he had always known he truly was, deep inside.

He watched her chest rise and fall, and her pulse beat in her neck. He saw emotions he could not name chase across her face. He was a man who waited for nothing and no one, save this woman…

And so he told himself he could wait a little longer now. Just a little longer.

"I… I don't understand," she said again, but her voice was little more than a whisper and there was that wild pulse in her neck, telling him the truth.

"I think you do understand," he said quietly. "I think you understand me entirely."

Though for the first time in his adult life, Lao Monteleone found himself wondering if a woman actually wanted him.

A notion so astounding, so impossible to conceive of, that if he hadn't been standing here—feeling an odd sensation that it took him long moments to recognize as a touch of *uncertainty*, another first—he would have laughed at the very idea.

As he watched, Chloe moistened her soft lips. She blinked, again and again, as if that might give her clarity.

"You have never given me any indication that you harbor these feelings," she said, with the tone and expression of someone wandering through a meadow who had only just realized she was weaving her way through land mines.

He could not say that he cared for it. More, it was not the reaction he had expected.

"I do not *harbor feelings*, Chloe," he said abruptly, as if he really was some kind of land mine and she had activated him with her misstepping. "Do not confuse this for mawkish poetry. You are already my wife. I am already your husband. This relationship has been in name only for far too long. All I am proposing is that we shift it."

"Shift it," she repeated, but when she blinked again, her gaze seemed to narrow.

"I am a remarkably busy man, as you know," he told her, not liking the way she was looking at him. "Why should I go through the trouble of divorcing you only to turn around and marry all over again to create legitimate heir. It's a waste of time and effort, surely, when you are here, have nothing better to do, and bonus—are already married. To me."

"Heaven forfend your time and effort be wasted," she murmured, her dark eyes narrowed further.

"There is no reason not to approach this efficiently," Lao told her as if he had never been more at his ease. "Efficiency and circumspection, that's all I ask."

"Efficiency." Her voice was changing, going up an octave with each syllable, and there was an unfamiliar gleam in her dark gaze. He had not seen it in a long while, but he suspected it was... temper? "Circumspection. And, of course, sex against walls, but let's gloss over that part."

That was the part he least wished to gloss over, but then, he had not anticipated that she would respond like this. He'd rather thought she would weep with gratitude the way she had when he'd married her five years ago and taken charge of all the details her father had left for her to handle. House, funds, bills, staff.

He could not see why this was hitting her so differently. Or why she'd imagined he would call her all the way to Sicily to divorce her when he could have her served with papers anywhere she happened to be—

Though he thought better of saying so.

"You already enjoy the benefits of my protection," he pointed out, quite reasonably, since it was true. "The only change for you will be the physical aspects of the relationship." He very nearly let himself smile, then. "But I flatter myself that you will not find what I require of you too onerous."

Chloe held his gaze for a long moment, and there was something almost electric about it. It seared into him, making him tense. Making him think it was wiser to set the absurdly delicate teacup aside. But then she wrenched her eyes from his and looked down into her lap. He followed her gaze and saw how she gripped her hands before her. Twisting her fingers together, as if agitated.

Lao could not conceive of a single reason why she should feel even the slightest hint of agitation. Not when he—*he*, Lao Monteleone himself— was standing before her, offering her something most women would kill to experience. It was not vanity that made him think so, he knew. It was a simple fact.

Perhaps she was overwhelmed, he reasoned. Perhaps it had never occurred to her that he might make such a generous offer. She likely had to pull herself together, for she was no longer eighteen and might imagine it was childish to weep the way she had, throwing herself into his arms and sobbing until she'd soaked the front of his shirt.

He waited, certain that in a moment she would look up again, wreathed in soft and yielding smiles, and accept what could only be seen as a remarkably generous offer on his part.

Again.

Because as irritating as he might have found it to think that she had expected him to divorce her today, he could concede that it would have been a reasonable expectation in a situation such as theirs.

This, however, was a gift.

Chloe looked up then, but there was no smile. No hint of moisture in her gaze. It was as if she had turned into a stranger before his very eyes. It was almost as if he didn't recognize her, so dark was her gaze, so oddly set was her jaw.

"No," she said.

Too distinctly for his taste. Too definitively.

That word seemed to squat there between them,

as if she'd tossed it into the middle of the room tied to a rock.

Lao realized he could not recall the last time someone had said no to him, either.

She was a revelation. Not one he entirely enjoyed. "I beg your pardon?"

"No," she said again, and then blew out a breath as if she was trying to control her reaction. Or steady herself. "I will have to refuse."

Lao waited, but she did not elaborate. Instead, she looked at him for moment, then rose, looking as if she meant to march straight back out of the room. And possibly the house.

He was beginning to tire of all this novelty.

"You do not intend to tell me why you have chosen to refuse me?" he asked, sounding almost lazy. Which she could not possibly know was Lao at his most dangerous.

Chloe stopped walking toward the door, but she did not turn back around to face him.

"If you would like a woman to have sex with you at your convenience," she said in a low voice that he hardly recognized, so different was it from how she normally spoke to him—all stammers and blushes, "I'm sure that you can find any number of them. But none of them will be me."

As if he had asked her to be his whore. He, who had done nothing but protect her for years.

Even going so far as to offer her the great honor of becoming the mother of the next generation of Monteleones. Lao could not account for what he was hearing.

Though he realized he had, indeed, heard her speak in a tone like this before. When she had been a cross little girl.

He didn't care for the memory.

Just as he didn't care for the way she stood there before him, her spine straight and her shoulders set in an indignant line.

He did not like it. He would not tolerate it.

"I think you have misunderstood me, Chloe," he said with a soft menace he did not attempt to hide. "It was not a request."

CHAPTER THREE

CHLOE COULD BARELY BREATHE. Her lungs seem to be working overtime, but she couldn't manage to get in a full breath. Every single nerve within her was alight, making her shake, deep down, in places she couldn't name.

Because for a moment…just for a moment… she had thought Lao had meant something completely different.

Something that had made everything inside her blaze hot and wild, like a comet leaving trails across the night sky—

But she should have known better.

A man like Lao did not have feelings, and certainly not for her. He had minions. And all he was proposing today was that she become one of them.

And then, while she was at it, produce no less than four children—the old-fashioned way—to follow his orders right along with her.

Later, perhaps, she would think about what

she'd imagined he was saying today, and let the full force of the emotions she felt come out. Or let herself name them. But not here, where he could see her. She hoped she would never have so little pride.

If that was all she was left with today, it would be enough. Chloe told herself it would have to be enough.

She had been *so close*. So close to that fluttery, shivery dream inside of her that she'd pretended not to have for more years than she could name. So close that for a moment, she had seen the unvarnished truth of who she was. Who she had always been, perhaps.

Worse still, the truth of what she felt about Lao. What, deep down, she thought she might always have wanted from him—even back before she had the vocabulary to express it.

Or the ability to look at any of these things directly.

Things she would have said she didn't even know how to express *now*, and for a moment, she hadn't needed to worry about what she could or couldn't manage to say because it seemed as if he was saying it all for her. As if he was taking care of that for her, too. The way he taken care everything else. For all these years.

She should have known better.

Truly, Chloe thought, she really should have *known*, and that she hadn't expected this at all was galling.

More than galling, if she was honest with herself about him, for once. It hurt.

It *hurt* that he wanted nothing more from her than for her to act as his convenient broodmare.

It was not a request, he'd just said, and that hurt too.

All of this hurt a whole lot more than she'd thought it would. Even when she'd thought he was divorcing her. At least a divorce made sense. This was…too close and too far away from too many things she should have known better than to entertain. Especially here.

No matter what he'd said to her.

"I want you in my bed every night," he had said.

And she'd thought… God, what she'd thought and what she'd *felt*.

In a bed. Against the wall. Anywhere and everywhere.

Like all her dreams were coming true—but she should have known better. She should have remembered that she wasn't the girl whose dreams came true. She was the girl who had a mother who wanted nothing to do with her and had lost everyone on this planet she'd ever loved.

Save one, but he was…

Well, he was impossible, and she knew that. She had always known it. As a child she'd thought of Lao as an *immensity*, not a man, as huge and overshadowing as a mountain.

Now she knew that the truth was far more complicated. He was all the things she'd imagined he was back then. But he was *also* a man, and that made everything…delicate.

Inside you, maybe, a tart voice inside piped up. *He seems anything but.*

Chloe turned, then.

And the expression on Lao's face made everything inside her go still. Then begin to…hum.

As if she was a tiny little creature, nothing more than prey, and he had her in his sights.

What she couldn't understand was the part of her that wanted nothing more than to be what he chased. And better yet, caught.

That seemed to land in her too hard, because Chloe felt something like winded.

"You don't control me, Lao," she said, and hated that her voice was far softer than it should have been. She made herself stand taller, as if a straight back would take the place of the spine she should have grown years ago.

She told herself there was no time like the present.

Lao only gazed at her, his hard face a study in arrogance. "Do I not?"

Chloe couldn't get her head around what was happening. How different this was from what she imagined. What she'd expected today.

The Lao who stood, slowly, before her was familiar in a thousand ways, and yet a stranger all the same. She should have been appalled. Offended, even. But she felt nothing so simple.

The way he looked at her was pitiless. She found that everything inside of her seemed to pull tight and then hold. Making it almost impossible to breathe.

Or do much of anything else, for that matter, like give voice to some of the things swirling around and around inside her and seeming to settle there, low in her belly.

"You can defy me if you wish," he said. In a tone she might have been tempted to believe was offhand if she hadn't been looking at him. If she hadn't been too able to see the intensity in his gaze.

"Thank you for your permission," she said, and felt fleetingly proud of how close to scathing she sounded.

"But what will become of you, Chloe?" he asked in that same low, deceptively casual manner at total odds with that glimmering steel gaze. "I think you'll find it a Pyrrhic victory at best. I control your funds. Here, on the grounds of this estate, I control your body. You cannot leave without my permission. Even if I did allow you to go, I could cut you off immediately and you would not have the necessary monies to make it to the sea. What then?"

"Are you really suggesting what I think you're suggesting?" She shook her head, but it didn't clear. Not even the slightest bit. "I feel as if I've stepped into an alternate universe."

"It is more that you have finally woken up, *dusci mia.*" He had never called her that before. It made the concrete beneath her feet seem to buckle and she didn't even know what it meant. "You have finally opened your eyes and seen what has been in front of you all this time."

She felt something move inside of her, blooming outward like some kind of internal tsunami. Fury, perhaps, though she wasn't sure that she'd ever experienced a fury like this, a burning, melting heat that coursed through her and seemed to glow, deep in her core. She was terribly afraid there was something more to it. Something more like grief.

"I thought you were my friend," she said quietly, though it was a fight to sound so calm. So… unbothered by what was happening here.

Because it was true that she had often imagined he might be her friend. That being his friend was the most she'd hoped for, even if there was that glowing thing inside her every time she thought of him. It was also true that *friendship* was not all she had imagined when it came to him, and that the idea of making their marriage real in a physical sense when it could not be real in all the other ways she craved him…*hurt*.

And she had the sneaking suspicion he knew it.

That he knew every thought she'd ever had about him. Every dream. Every stray notion.

She told herself what she felt then was horror, but it was much too hot for that to be true.

"Some would say I am the best friend you've ever had." He did not move closer to her, and yet she felt as if he had closed the distance between them and encircled her neck with one broad, hard hand. She felt that breathless. And as if he knew that, too, Lao thrust his hands in his pockets. It should have made him look more casual. It did not. "Have I not been at your beck and call these last five years? Have I not done everything you've asked of me? Can you think of a better friend to you than I?"

"How depressing it is to realize that even the great Lao Monteleone is only nice to a woman when he has an ulterior motive." She blinked away that great wave inside her, because it didn't matter what it was. Grief. Fury. That glowing thing she didn't want to look at directly. A kind of shame that she had let herself believe anything he said in the first place. That she had delivered herself directly into his hands.

That she had hoped, however briefly, that he might have been sharing something of himself with her when he'd said he wanted her to be his wife in full. That it might have meant something.

"I cannot make sense of this reaction, when it is clear that there has always been an attraction here," he said, though he did not sound the least bit insulted. But Chloe could not find that a good thing, because it meant only that he was a stranger to her here. The one she read about in the papers. The formidable opponent, on the few occasions he actually allowed others to note what he was doing, out there in power circles so lofty most didn't know they existed. More often, he was talked about as he might be some kind of ghost, forever moving in and out of the shadowy doors of power.

She had never recognized the Lao she knew in the accounts she'd read of him.

But she saw him now. As he spoke of *attraction* as if she was being childish for pretending otherwise. Or for wishing there was something less clinical in the way he said it. "Then we are both of us surprised. Because I cannot recognize my stepbrother in a man who would threaten me the way you have today."

For a moment he considered her, and she thought that just possibly, she might have gotten through to him—but then he laughed.

She would not describe it as mirthful.

"You must breathe rarefied air indeed if you find the notion of becoming my wife in full a *threat*, Chloe." That steel gray gleam became a part of the humming inside her, making it almost impossible to stand still. "I would be tempted to find this insulting, but the trouble is, I don't believe you."

"You don't..." She shook her head, ordering the clamor inside her to die down, though it only seemed to get louder. So she had to talk a little more fiercely "It's not a matter of *belief.* It's true you've controlled many things about my life for these past years, but it's *my* life. I thought you were helping me, not...collecting evidence to use against me like this!"

To her surprise, she found that he looked almost... proud. "And here I was beginning to think your personality died with your father, Chloe."

She felt as if he'd slapped her. Or perhaps she would've preferred it if he had. "Are you truly trying to use my father's death against me?"

It seemed as if he moved closer, or perhaps it was simply that he took over the whole room by just...existing. Especially when he shrugged, so languidly, as if none of this affected him at all.

Why that should bother her almost more than the rest was a question she did not intend to answer.

"I remember you as a child," he said, though he was not looking at her like she was a child. At all. "You said what you felt with little consideration for anyone around you or any false notions of courtesy. That is not a complaint. It was refreshing. But when you came here five years ago, it was as if you were lost at sea. And as far as I can tell, you have been lost ever since." She opened her mouth to defend herself, but there was something about the way his dark eyes gleamed that kept her from it. "You have no purpose, Chloe. You waft about aimlessly, from one pointless enterprise to the next. What is it now? You adorn some SoHo art gallery?"

"I'm an assistant, not an adornment."

"And how, precisely, do you assist? What do you know about art?"

"I know I like art, which is more than I can say for you."

"I cannot tell if you mean you do not think I like art myself, or if it is me you do not like," Lao said with ferocious unconcern. "But either way, it will not last. Whatever this enthusiasm is, it will end and you will wander into something else equally meaningless. What future do you see for yourself? Where do you think you will be in ten years?"

Chloe had no idea why she was shaking. She only knew that she was no longer containing that shaking inside of her, and that was a shame. Because he could no doubt see the way she trembled, and would likely attribute it to the wrong cause.

Or the right one, came that unflinching voice within her.

But no. She was certain it was fury. A deep, bracing, shivery and melting *fury*.

"It doesn't matter where I am in ten years," she told him, and she might have been trembling like a cursed fawn, but she couldn't remember the last time she'd been so *aware* of…well, everything. The way he looked at her, and the heat in it. The competing waves of emotion that buffeted her. That blaze inside her, bright and impossible to ignore. As if it had been waiting a long while to shine. "Because I came here for divorce. I thank you for looking out for me these past five years, even if it turns out you weren't doing any such thing. But I'm perfectly capable of handling my own affairs from here on out."

She thought that hit all the right notes, but Lao seemed unimpressed. He did not move, only considered her. "Are you? I don't think you have the slightest idea what your affairs entail. Do you have the slightest idea what it is I do for you?"

"I can figure it out."

"Because you are under the impression that you—lacking any kind of education and having spent these last years pretending to work at public relations or swanning about an art gallery because they find you pretty—are prepared to take the reins of a multinational corporation, with all its implications and financial considerations. To say nothing of your own personal fortune, about which you have never inquired, not even once, in the whole of the past five years I have managed it and grown it. Tell me, Chloe, do you even know what you're worth?"

She flushed then and knew it to be a corrosive kind of shame, the sort that might take her down to her knees if she let it. So she did the only thing she could. She opened her mouth and came out with a number she'd read in a gossipy magazine a year or so before.

And did not feel any better when Lao only shook his head as if he was disappointed in her, which was almost as bad as the rush of shame that she'd let this get so out of control. "You don't even know enough to know that I enjoy feeding numbers like that to amuse myself. I like to see what happens when I let go of certain balloons and let them rise. I like to see what goes where."

He let out a sound that was not quite a sigh, but it made her wish she could sink through the concrete floor and topple straight down into the wild heart of one of the canyons below them.

And he wasn't done. "Yet you stand here in my house and parrot my own fake numbers back to me. In the same breath as you try to tell me you're prepared to handle all that I have done for you yourself. I could let you do it, of course. I'm almost tempted to, because I know what you are perhaps too stubborn to see today." Again, that deep, bone-rattling gleam in his gaze that made everything feel precarious, even her own skin. "The only thing you will accomplish is wasting your own time, and then, later, mine. When you come crawling back to beg for my help once more."

"That, Lao, will never occur."

"Indeed, it will not." His voice was so dark, then. His gaze was so hard. "Because I have no intention of allowing any of that to happen."

"You're not thinking straight."

"Am I not?"

"No." Though Chloe knew she wasn't, either. Maybe there was no straight thinking to be had. Maybe she just hadn't noticed, too busy trying not to swallow her own tongue at the sight of him in that

bathing costume. Or the memory. She found her hands outstretched, palms up, imploring him, and wanted to hate herself for begging—but couldn't quite get there. Not under these impossible conditions. "You don't really want this. I know you don't."

"What interests me far more is why you think that you don't want it," he said. One of his dark brows rose, and there was the faintest hint of a curve in one corner of his mouth. "Do I disgust you?"

He did not look as if he was overly worried about how she might respond to that, so she knew she should tell him that he did. That she was *disgusted* with him. That the very notion of being *a true wife* to him revolted her, that she had never thought of him as anything but a kind of distant brother figure. She knew, instinctually, that if she said any of that, he would divorce her within the hour and she would never see him again.

Not ever.

All she needed to do was *say* it, and yet she couldn't. She couldn't bring herself to open her mouth and lie to him.

Especially not about that.

Not when the many ways she'd lied to herself over the years seemed so obvious to her now and more, throbbed insistently between her legs.

He only watched her, much too closely, while the space between them seemed to join in the throbbing she could feel all over her. It felt like a kind of madness.

There was something electric in the space between them. There was something almost terrifying.

"Because," Lao continued quietly, as if she'd answered him. As if she'd dared. "I would give you the same advice I gave you when you wanted to begin drinking spirits."

Chloe remembered that far too well. She had always liked when Lao gave her the full force of his brooding attention. She had been perhaps fourteen. The friend from boarding school she'd had with her that Christmas had gotten very drunk and silly, and Lao had taken it upon himself to make certain that she did not intend to behave in the same manner.

"Men get drunk all the time," Chloe had said crossly, because she had always been so *cross* then. And never afraid to show it. "Why is it the end of the world if a girl does too?"

"Because the world is unfair," Lao had replied with his typical bluntness. "Drunk boys tend to be loutish. Drunk girls, by contrast, easily turn into victims. One way to avoid this is to never drink beyond elegance, Chloe. And never seek oblivion."

She hadn't wanted to tell him that she was always the one who was careful in her group of friends. The one who never allowed herself to get as foolish as the rest. She'd thought it would make her seem unsophisticated, and she had dearly wanted him to find her anything at all but that.

"If in doubt," Lao had told her quietly over the sounds of the grand party in the distance and her friend moaning on the bathroom floor in the next room, "I would advise you to sample whatever it is everyone else is drinking, but sparingly. How can you know if you like it otherwise?"

"How does anyone know if they like anything?" she had demanded, but she had been breathless by then. That was what he did to her, and much too easily. Even back then.

He had not smiled. He did not smile, not Lao, but she had felt as if he had. And in any case, he had reached over and tapped the very tip of her nose.

"Mind you, never drink anything you don't see opened and poured with your own eyes, please."

Yet what she remembered was not the advice, but that tap. And how she had felt burned alive by a casual touch that he could just as easily have used on a pet cat.

But he didn't, she remembered telling herself,

lying awake much later while her friend snored. *He touched* me *instead*.

Like it meant something.

"I can see you remember as well as I do," he said now, and his words seemed engraved into her bones. As he wasn't speaking to her, but from within her. Once again, he didn't smile. Once again, there was only that faint suggestion of a curve in the corner of his sensually stern lips. "I'm not going to club you over the head, Chloe. Or drag you off to my cave like a Neanderthal. But I would invite you to sample what I am offering before you dismiss it out of hand. Is that so terrible? Do you think that deserves the level of drama we have seen here today?"

She could tell that he was being deliberately condescending. That he wanted to provoke her, and he was succeeding. What she didn't understand was why she didn't simply turn around again and march off. She could put it to the test, couldn't she? She could see if it was true that she couldn't escape his estate without his permission.

But she didn't move.

"I think of you as a brother," she lied, when she never had. Not really. He had always been more to her. Always. "Nothing more."

"I don't think that you do."

He did move closer then.

And Chloe felt her pulse take over the whole of her body. As if it changed her where she stood, making her the pulse itself. Part of that gleaming way he gazed at her.

Proving what a liar she'd turned out to be, that easily.

"I don't think you know me better than I do," she threw at him, maybe a little too fiercely. "I don't even know why you would think that you could. You hardly know me as it is."

"Chloe, you are my wife." Lao's voice was too intense. It moved within her like a kind of smoke. It wound around and around inside her, making it impossible to think of anything else. As if it filled her up. As if it had already changed her on some fundamental level it made her shiver to consider. "You might have spent these last years lost, but I have not. I have always known exactly where you are. And exactly who you are."

Her mouth worked. She swallowed, hard. "You followed me?"

"I have protected you in every possible way I could," he shot back at her, his voice rough. "Just as I promised you that I would."

He came even closer and then he reached out.

At last, something in her whispered.

Then he made it worse—or better—and smoothed a hand over the fall of her hair.

And there was something about the way he did that. So softly, when everything he'd said so far was hard. Demanding.

So softly that she found herself trembling all over again.

"Lao," she whispered. "I…"

"Dusci mia," he murmured, that big hand of his warm against the side of her face. Like sunshine in his palm. "Kiss me."

CHAPTER FOUR

CHLOE WANTED TO RUN.

But not away from Lao. *Into him*, if such a thing was possible.

His hand was so warm, the look in his eyes so commanding, she almost thought it was. That he would make it so.

Everything inside of her felt stretched out between those two extremes—his hand and his gaze—as if they were extremes in the first place instead of simply Lao Monteleone in all his considerable glory.

She wanted so badly to fight this. To fight *herself*.

Not because she didn't want him. But because she did. Oh, how she did.

And this, she understood, was not likely to be a tap on the nose, like she was nothing more than a house pet.

She would never know how it was that she had

stood here all this time, pretending that what upset her was the notion of making their relationship real. When the truth was, what bothered her more was that she might lose herself in all these feelings she had so deliberately kept at bay all these years. Feelings she had resolutely refused to name.

What if she lost herself, getting entirely swept away, while he was unaffected?

The very notion was unbearable—

But Lao's hand was on her cheek. His eyes were so stern, so compelling.

And Chloe, for once, did not feel the slightest bit lost.

On the contrary. She had never felt more *found* than she did right now.

It was as if she had never had any other choice but this.

She eased herself forward, her heart drumming so hard in her chest that it actually *hurt*. Then she reached out a hand so she could balance it— gingerly—on the sheer rock wall of his astonishing chest.

For a moment, Chloe could only stand there, amazed at her own temerity. Or maybe what truly amazed her was the way so simple and light a touch seemed to rebound back into her. Lighting her up.

Making her glow from within.

Some part of her—maybe all of her—expected him to take control. Maybe she wanted him to. Bend his head, sweep her into his arms, carry her off...

Maybe she assumed that he would do exactly that.

But for all his talk of keeping her here, and all his threats—implied and direct—Lao did nothing.

He merely waited.

And, second by second, that made everything more intense. More electric.

It seemed to take Chloe an age or three to lift her gaze from where it rested, there on the hand that nestled between the planes of his hard pectoral muscles. She could feel the heat of his skin. His *body*.

And something about the simple wonder of that, of him, was so erotic it made her feel near enough to giddy.

She could have stood there, just like that, forever.

But Lao had told her to kiss him. And she knew that it was unlikely she would make it through another day if she did not obey him.

Because deep down, there was the truth that somehow Lao had known all along.

It was that Chloe had wanted to kiss this

man—and do a good deal more than merely *kiss* him—forever.

Even when he had been her lofty stepbrother, always clearly in a state of deep disapproval over his mother's choice to remarry.

And even if, left her own devices, she would never have admitted such a thing. That didn't make it untrue. It didn't change the inexorable pull she felt now, so close to him at last. *Touching him*, after all these years. It was so overwhelming she wanted to simply…close her eyes and disappear into him.

Instead, she lifted her head and let his magnetism guide her. Pull her.

Take her over.

So that it seemed only natural to bring her head up, then go up on her toes so she could angle herself against him. Into him.

Then, and only then, could she strain up that last little bit to press her mouth to his.

And for a stretch of time that could have been a second or an eternity, that was all there was.

The press of her lips to his. The scent of him, spice and sunshine. The way her own heart was a jarring force in her chest, a deep thunder she could feel washing through her, over her, and making a ruckus in the strangest places. Spiraling around and around and shooting out a kind of spun gold into all the recesses of her body only to settle with great heat between her legs.

Making all the rest of her seem to glow.

Chloe surged against him, desperate and seeking and *wanting* things she didn't even know how to name. *More*, whispered something inside of her. She just wanted *more*, whatever that was. Whatever it looked like, felt like—as long as it was Lao.

And when his hands shifted at last, guiding her mouth where he wanted it to and allowing him to change the angle and the slick slide of their lips against one another, it was as if something in her began to sing.

She couldn't forget, not even for a moment, that this was Lao.

This was Lao. Her Lao.

This was *Lao*, and he was *licking* his way along the seam of her lips, then dipping inside. She was stroking her tongue against his, following his lead. And she couldn't tell what was more intoxicating— his taste that flooded her mouth and her senses, or the sensation itself, or the fact that this was happening at all.

His other arm came around her back and held her there as he leaned in, so she was no longer on her tiptoes but bent back into his hold.

And he kissed her, again and again, and she kissed him back.

And it was Lao, and this was *them*, and too many things made sense to her now, colliding inside her with every new slide of his tongue.

The dreams she'd had for years. How she'd gone out of her way to contrive to be near him, no matter how flimsy the excuse.

Even here, five years ago, she had come running as if he was the only man on earth. The only *person*.

As if Lao alone could help her.

He kissed her and he kissed her. And it was fire and it was light. It was golden and it was heat.

It was far, far better than all the things she'd pretended she hadn't been imagining since she was much younger than she was now.

Chloe wanted to dance in the flame of this forever. She wanted to crawl along the length of him, to swing herself into his arms, to strip them both of all the clothes they wore so she could get her skin all over his.

And then see what happened.

When he set her away from him, there was still that hard gleam in his gaze. There was also the hint of a deep triumph over his face, but she didn't mind that as perhaps she should.

Because she was feeling triumphant herself.

Because for a moment—just the faintest moment before his typical harshness took hold—the great Lao Monteleone looked just as shaken as she felt.

In the next instant it was gone, but Chloe decided she would hold on to it anyway. She would hoard the memory of that scant little breath of time, because even if she'd only imagined it, well. It still felt like everything.

It still felt like the kind of treasure she'd long since stopped believing she might ever find.

He smoothed his hand over her hair once more. Though this time, when he finished, he brought his fingers down the side of her face. And his thumb diverted from the line of her jaw to trace her lower lip.

"I think we will do nicely," he said in a low voice.

He did not sound as if that was up for debate.

And Chloe meant to argue. She did. If only because he shouldn't make such assumptions... But somehow, she couldn't get that message from her brain to her mouth, and that triumphant look on his face only intensified.

Another bolt of heat seemed to simmer there between them, but Chloe stepped away. She had to *make* herself step away from all that brooding heat and steel gray intensity.

And she really didn't know if she wanted to start spinning herself around in circles, like a little girl gone giddy, or if really, she wanted nothing more than to curl up in a ball and sob out all these messy feelings churning inside her.

But either way, didn't matter. Because clearly, Lao saw what happened between them as capitulation on her part. He moved past her, stepping out into the hall and summoning his staff, issuing instructions in rapid Italian. Only then did he look at her once more.

"You will need to settle in," he told her, and she noted that he did not ask her if she'd *like* to settle in. He was telling her to go and do it while he did whatever it was he did here—like run the world from his mountaintop, presumably. And again, she wanted to argue, but her mouth no longer felt like hers. She could taste him on her tongue. She could *taste him* and all she could do was stare back at him, wondering why no one had ever told her that kissing a man like Lao could make her whole, entire body feel like someone else's. Like his. "My staff will see to any needs you might have, Chloe, and we will meet again this evening."

He did not wait for her to comment on that. Much less mount any sort of argument. He turned and started back across the great expanse of the room toward his desk while Chloe was politely swept off by a waiting phalanx of his servants.

She wasn't sure she really came back to herself until they were walking down a corridor she'd never been in before, all modern lines and expansive white space to show off the edgy modern art that somehow worked in this ancient setting. Before she could comment on the juxtaposition of old and new, they were beckoning her into a grand suite of rooms that she knew at once belonged to Lao.

It all belonged to him, obviously. But this was where he *lived*.

The last time she had stayed here, it had been in the lovely, cheerful guest apartments, all bright yellows and blues and polished antiques.

This was something else again. The art gallery feel of the hall gave way to a great deal of old stone and dark wood that somehow contrasted beautifully with so many sweeping windows and French doors that opened out over the island, letting in the sky and the mountains and, far off in the distance, the sea.

Chloe assumed they would drop her here and then, no doubt, lock her away until Lao was ready for her. Instead, she found herself surrounded by a set of female attendants, who very happily took it upon themselves to buff and shine every part of her.

They removed the varnish from her toes and fingers, and then reapplied it in a gleaming red.

She was led into a room with a massage table, where aestheticians worked over her. First a bit of waxing, then a facial, then a massage to soothe it all away.

Chloe had always liked a spa. She and her friends had been to some lovely ones. But she couldn't recall ever having had a private spa arranged all around her before. It would have been overwhelming, she reckoned, if she wasn't so boneless.

Hours passed before it occurred to her to realize that this wasn't a gift that Lao was giving *her*.

He was preparing his own gift.

He was preparing her for later.

That made her so weak, everywhere, that she was happy she was already lying down.

Eventually, they led her into her bedroom at last. She expected to find Lao there, but it was empty. And more than that, she could tell with a glance that it wasn't his.

She didn't know how she knew that, but she was certain all the same. It was a pretty enough room, with a canopied bed, an antique chaise, and a selection of priceless furniture kept in pristine condition. One door led to a large, sprawling bathroom suite with a great big copper tub in a glass alcove. Another led to a dressing room that looked like a high-end Marylebone boutique, but it was through a different door entirely that she found what she was looking for.

Another bedroom, next to hers. Separated by not only that dressing room for her, but one on his side as well, filled with beautiful clothes that smelled of his sunshine and spices.

Chloe understood at once that Lao had placed her in the bedchamber adjoining his, the way men of his station like to do with their wives. "Only peasants share their grubby little queen beds," one of her friends had said once—the sort of joke that wasn't a joke at all.

And Lao was no peasant.

She knew she'd found his actual bedroom immediately. It was more masculine, for a start, than her canopied bed and floral accents. But more than that, there was some faint hint of that same scent that told her it was his. Some little hint that made every part of her seem to shiver.

Especially when she looked at that big, wide bed that commanded most of the space against one wall.

It took her a long while to get her breath back to normal.

She went back into the room that had been allocated for her on polished feet that felt unsteady beneath her. Once there, she made her way to the grand windows so she could stand there and gaze out at the rolling hills of the Monteleone estate, spread out there for her.

Her breath was closer to normal, but it took longer still to make all that giddiness and sensation subside. She would nearly get there and then she would think, *I am his gift* and it would start all over again.

But eventually she managed to tamp it all down just enough she could think straight. Or try.

She hadn't expected this. She'd come down this weekend because he'd asked, and she'd been sure she knew exactly what she was walking into. She'd expected divorce papers and perhaps a polite dinner. She'd intended to express her gratitude and be back in London by noon the following day.

There was no way she could have expected his proposal that they make this marriage *real*.

Much less that kiss.

God. That kiss.

But she couldn't lose herself in that wave of sensation again. Not yet.

Chloe tried to think critically, never her strong point. And certainly not when in Lao's direct orbit.

But surely there was no real reason that she couldn't make this marriage work. For her as well as for him. Lao wasn't the only one who could expect to get what he liked out of this. *Four* children, for God's sake.

She had always intended to have children, the way everyone seemed to *intend* to have them—in a very distant way, set off sometime in the future. Not *now*. But she didn't have to worry about that no matter what Lao had planned, because every three months, without fail, she went and got a shot of birth control in her hip. Not because she'd ever put it to the test, but because she'd always thought that at any moment she might decide it was time to begin a wild and crazy sort of life.

Chloe had been waiting to make that particular decision for a long while. Because it turned out that Lao was the only man she'd ever met who could call up this kind of response in her. She couldn't deny that it was thrilling. It was every silly fantasy she'd ever had, finally coming true in the form of that kiss—and whatever came next.

She felt that heat in her again, winding tight and yet managing to reach every part of her at once so she couldn't think of anything to do but lay her forehead against the cool glass. And think about the fact that while she fully intended to surrender to whatever this marriage, in name only until today, brought her, she also knew she could do it fully only because she didn't need to worry about the very consequences Lao claimed to want.

He might think he knew her every move, but she had to think that wasn't entirely true. Because she'd seen her doctor for her three-month shot only last week, which meant that she had three months to explore whatever happened here without having to worry about getting pregnant. Three months to see how she felt about this man who only wanted heirs when she wanted...so much more. But she couldn't help thinking that if Lao knew that she couldn't get pregnant right away, he wouldn't have started this. If he really did know everything about her, why would he have begun this now?

What that meant to Chloe was that she could... throw herself into this. She could chase down every last one of these daydreams she'd hardly ever admitted she had. She could finally see what all the great fuss was about, and then, if she didn't like any part of this, she could leave.

Because she could lull him into a false sense of security. She had no doubt of that. He was so sure of himself. Better yet, he was so sure of *her*. He would expect her to fall in line because she always did, and because that was what everyone did in his presence.

So there was no reason at all she couldn't let him think that.

For as long as it was convenient.

Then do exactly as she pleased. But this time, without wondering what it was she was missing.

Later, the staff descended upon her again and

bore her off with great flourish to the dressing room where they made as if to start outfitting her for the evening.

"These aren't my clothes," Chloe said, stopping short in the doorway.

"Mr. Monteleone wanted to make sure you have as many options as possible," one of the women said. She smiled knowingly. "He is so generous."

Her fingers found their way to her own lips, then. Teasing out the leftover sensation of Lao's kiss that only seemed to get deeper as the hours passed. She would have expected the opposite— but it was as if the kiss had spent the day settling deep into her flesh, becoming part of her.

Doing what Lao did so well and changing her from the inside out.

She reminded herself that she was reclaiming the situation.

"He is very generous," she had to agree, and she even smiled. "But I can trust myself tonight."

As lines in the sand went, it seemed silly. Pointless, even. But she'd drawn it and she would stand by it, Chloe thought. She needed to remember that it had started off like this. That his kiss had sent her spinning, perhaps, but she was still *herself*.

She didn't know what she expected after her announcement. The team of women who gazed back at her to fight her on this, perhaps? Instead, they all smiled and nodded as if they'd expected this all along.

"As you wish, Madam," the same woman said. "We will simply enhance your natural beauty, shall we?"

What that meant, Chloe discovered, was that when she pulled out the simple, workhorse of a black dress she wore to everything—because it could be crumpled up into a ball and tossed into the bowels of any given suitcase, but still look chic and unmarred with a single shake—the women gathered around her transformed what she thought of as a certain quiet pulled togetherness into elegance. They did something understated yet complicated with her hair, twisting the dark mass of it back and fastening it to the nape of her neck, so that it looked deceptively simple and breathtakingly sophisticated. They smudged shadow on her eyelids and dusted something like gold over her cheekbones until she looked as if she was lit up from within.

They capped it off with a hint of diamonds at her ears, her neck, and one wrist. And would not hear of it when she protested. They even switched out her shoes for something a bit flashier, and then shooed her from the bedchamber with a whole lot of Italian and laughter, making it clear that they would not let her back inside.

So there was nothing for it but to head down-stairs to dinner.

Where Lao would be waiting for her.

Everything seemed to spin around and around inside of her then, building up that heat that had stayed at a constant simmer throughout the day.

She felt nervous, she realized as she walked down the long hallway again and found her way to a stair that led her down to the castle's main level. Where, she knew, there were any number of little salons and dining halls as befit the grand place this must have been in the past and was again now.

But all she could think about was Lao.

Once again, she got glimpses of herself in the mirror as she passed. She could see the flush of excitement on her cheeks and the indisputable art-istry that the women had practiced on the rest of her, making her shimmer as she moved.

She couldn't tell if she felt like an elegant bride, or a sacrifice.

Why not both? a voice inside her asked.

And she laughed a bit at that, only to swallow it down hurriedly when she turned the corner to go down the last flight of the grand stair, because Lao was there at the foot—his steel gray gaze slam-ming into her so hard she had to stop and regain her balance.

But it didn't occur to her to stay there where she

stopped. She started moving again as soon as she was steady, as if she was helpless to do anything but go to him.

Not helpless, she lectured herself. *Curious.*

And it was as if she was gliding, caught up in that dark heat he aimed her way, all the way down to the bottom step.

Where he took her hand at last.

And for what seemed like forever, simply held it.

"Truly," he said, in that low voice of his that wound around and around inside her, "you are a thing of beauty, Chloe."

She had never before felt beautiful. Not like this. Not when all she could see was that frank male appraisal, and feel all of that dark, stirring heat inside her.

She had never before *believed* that she was beautiful, but she believed him. She believed he thought so. She could feel the truth of it.

Lao was wearing one of those dark suits that was hand-tailored to the exact width of his shoulders, the precise leanness of his hips.

"So are you, Lao," she said softly, then found herself smiling when he looked surprised that she should compliment him in return.

It made her wonder if he was so overwhelming, so wildly intense, and so astronomically remote in every way that mattered, that no one bothered to offer him compliments. But any such thoughts splintered, because he carried her hand to his lips and pressed a courtly sort of kiss to her knuckles.

It should have made her laugh. It should have felt silly and old-fashioned, but it didn't. Not in an ancient castle, perched here above an island so steeped in history.

And not when the faint brush of his lips across the back of her hand made everything inside her seemed to curl up tight, then begin to boil.

"Welcome, little one," he murmured, the heat in his gaze making everything inside her take notice, especially the tender flesh between her legs. And that heart of hers that would not stop its wild thundering. "To our wedding night. At last."

CHAPTER FIVE

LAO HAD SPENT the whole of the day distracted, which was unacceptable on every level. The point of having a wife, as his father had always told him, was so that a man could focus *more*, not less.

"Too many men's lives are wasted in the pursuit of women," the old man had told his son when Lao was barely thirteen. "And who can begrudge a man a judicious sowing of oats, wild or otherwise? But a wise man settles on a wife early so he can turn his attention to things that matter."

Meaning, things other than Lao's mother. But for all that Lao knew that his father had been the sort of old-school figure who would have done well in a previous century or two—and who hadn't been kind to the wife he'd settled on—he also knew that a man in his position needed to pay attention to his work. A little eccentricity was permitted, even encouraged.

But the moment he lost focus was the moment

the Monteleone reputation could suffer a critical hit. Once that happened, the work of centuries of his ancestors could be gone. Just like that.

Power was perception before it was anything else. His father had taught him that, too.

Lao had finally concluded—halfway through a phone call he had hardly heard a word of and could not have recalled if his life depended on it—that it was part and parcel of this waiting that he had been doing for far too long now.

But the waiting was at an end.

And he intended to enjoy tonight in every possible way.

It helped the Chloe looked like a dream come true. And that, better still, she looked at him as if she felt the same. He led her through the castle's great halls, but did not take her to the grand dining room, because tonight he was after something far more intimate. Something memorable and even a bit magical, come to that. He walked her outside and then down a well-lit path that followed what remained of the castle's old walls, hugging the side of the cliff.

"This used to be a stop along the soldiers watch each night," he told her as he led her around to the remains of a medieval tower, the one that sat on the furthest edge of the cliff that stretched out over the slope of the mountainside. "They could see any enemies coming from far off."

"And then fight them?" Chloe asked.

Lao slanted to look down at her. "One of the great boons of Castello Monteleone is that its position is such that a great many fights could be avoided before they occurred. Some generations of my forebears simply barricaded themselves here and kept the mountain roads impassable, so that any enemies who might have wished to confront them died out before they did."

That was not the strictest interpretation of his family's history, but it was true enough.

And Chloe smiled. "Here I thought that Sicily was stitched together entirely of blood feuds."

"Vendettas are as life, *ovviamente*. No Sicilian would ever tell you otherwise. But those stitches fall apart if none of the offending blood remains. My family has always preferred the longer view."

He took the last turn in the path and was perhaps more pleased that he should have been when he heard her indrawn breath beside him. And when he turned, he saw the look of pleasure that washed over her face.

And liked it a bit more than he should if his only goal was *focus*—but he shoved that unhelpful notion aside.

Because the tower he had brought Chloe to was

a ruin, but it had been transformed according to his specifications. His staff had strung up too many lanterns to count from what was left of the roof, taking advantage of the temperate evening to create a dinner for two, here not quite beneath the stars on this warm night.

Lao was not a romantic. There had never been a call for such sentimentality, not in the whole of his life.

But it did not take much to understand that Chloe, dreamy and lost Chloe, was nothing but.

He led her to the table and took his time settling her into the seat that waited there. He sat opposite her, across the cozy table he had requested.

"This is magical," she said in a hushed sort of voice, looking around. There were candles on every possible surface, flickering in the night breeze. Tapestries hung over the holes in what once had been walls on three sides of the remains of the tower, leaving the fourth wall open. Letting in the sweet Sicilian air, the sparkling night sky, and the sea far off in the distance.

The little sigh Chloe let out sounded like music.

"Molto bene," Lao murmured, and then inclined his head toward the shadows where his staff waited, so that the meal would begin in earnest.

And then he set about an enterprise that was entirely new to him. Seduction.

As they ate the pine delicacies his staff had prepared, he played with her hand. He leaned closer. He listened intently to every word she said, asking her question after question. He made her laugh. He made her consider her replies. By the time their big plates were served, she looked more caught up in him than any meal.

What he had not considered was the possibility that he, too, might feel as caught up in her.

"You must feel out of step with the world up here," she said at one point, her gaze out toward the stars. When she turned back to him, she seemed to have them in her eyes. "Or maybe that's what you like about it?"

"I do not worry much about keeping time with the world." But he softened his tone. "It is not arrogance to suggest that the world keeps time with me, whether they know it or not."

Chloe laughed. "No, not arrogance. Not from you, Lao. Perish the thought."

And he had never wooed a woman in his life. Normally all he needed to do was glance at a woman and she would follow him about until he was no longer interested.

But for this one, he would make an exception to all his usual rules.

He felt it was the least he could do on this, their

wedding night. To this woman who was already his wife.

So he did not comment on the fact that she dared *tease* him. *Him.* Instead, he asked her question about her art gallery. Not about what, exactly, she thought she was doing there. That could wait. But rather what drew her to an art gallery in the first place.

Chloe sat back in her chair and smiled as if she was truly happy. Not that Lao had much of a reference point. Happiness was the province of lesser men, or so his father had always told him.

"This is the most excited I can remember seeing you in some time," he told her after she'd gone on for some time about the *feelings* art kicked up in her. When all he could really focus on was the sensation that surged in him whenever she leaned closer to make a point. "It seems you really do like art, after all."

"You have quite a bit of art," she said, one hand playing with the stem of her wine glass. Her hair had begun to come out of its twists, so that tempting tendrils fell about her face, begging for his fingers. So he reached over to twist one tendril around and around his finger. To watch the way her eyes lit up as he did, then went unfocused.

"The place is stuffed full of art," he agreed,

though he was surprised he could track the conversation. "It's hard to keep track of it all."

That, too, was not exactly true. His father had felt strongly that Lao needed to know every single piece of what was his, or how else could he protect it? His education had required a great many tours through the family collections, even back when this castle was little more than a moldering old ruin on the edge of the property.

"But do you *enjoy* the art you have stuffed into every nook and cranny?" Chloe asked with the sort of intensity he found made him think of what she would be like in bed. This fierce, he hoped. This laser-focused on her need. And his. "When you pass one of the Great Masters that simply hangs about, mostly unseen, one of your walls, do you pause? Are you swept up in the glory of it? Or do you take more pride simply in the owning of it?"

He studied her, letting go of that tendril of her hair and watching as it felt against her cheek. He could not have said what that faint sense of something like unease that crawled through him, then. "I appreciate all the things I collect. Or I would not trouble myself to collect them."

And he could see that look in her dark eyes. He could read the question there as surely as if she'd asked it, though she hadn't. Perhaps it was the magic of this night. Perhaps she simply did not dare.

"Appreciation is not the same thing," Chloe told him with more of a serious tone than he would have thought a discussion of his art collection required. She even frowned at him. "Art is supposed to sweep you away, or what's the point of it? If it's nothing but a balance sheet, why bother with it at all?"

"We are speaking of *art*, yes? I wish to be certain."

The wind had made her bold, he could see. And there was a part of him that wanted to tap that down at once, because he knew where that led, that sort of irrepressible spirit. He had watched his mother try to bloom in the same circumstances, and fail.

But there was another part of him that liked it.

Even the way she waved a hand, dismissively, as if she expected him to argue with her. Or maybe wanted him to. What was curious was that he did. "Yes, whatever art is to you. Blah-blah-blah investments, I imagine. But, Lao." She leaned forward again, that intense expression on her face once more. "What *stirs your soul*? What makes you feel *alive*?"

And she had never sounded so naive to him. So filled with that fervor and certainty that he should have laughed. He should have told her that reality had nothing to do with souls and he should know, as he spent most of his days shaping it.

Yet he found, to his surprise, that his sex was deeply interested in all this talk of passion.

"Perhaps you can teach me," he said instead.

Her dark eyes searched his, as if looking for trick. Then a smile moved over her mouth, reminding him of her taste. And reigniting the bright flame of his hunger. "Perhaps I can."

"Do I disappoint you, little one?" Lao asked softly. "Did you imagine we could light our own sparks here, speaking of oils and canvas?"

Her breath seemed to take her a moment. "You asked me why I liked working in the art gallery. I'm telling you, Lao. That's all."

Then he watched her close up before him, like some kind of spring flower deprived of sunshine. Like he'd hurt her feelings. But *feelings* should have had nothing to do with this. This was about sex and the heirs he required.

And, too, this was about wanting her, when he had never wanted anything.

When he had never been given the experience of *having* to want.

But the part of him that was only and ever the man who wanted his hands on her perfect body, and his sex so deep inside her that he was tempted to forget his own august name, was perfectly happy to show her passion, too.

Better passion than feelings, he thought then.

He pushed back in his seat, enjoying the way her eyes widened as he rose. "I prefer a far different canvas, Chloe."

He did not wait for her to comment on that. He could not *wait* a moment more. Instead, Lao reached over, lifted her from her seat, and drew her over his lap.

And he didn't wait for her to settle against him, he simply claimed her mouth with his.

This time, he asserted himself.

This time, he feasted on her, the way he had watched her feast on the art from his kitchens tonight. And she tasted heady indeed, wine and rich foods, and beneath it all, that taste that had driven him mad all day. That taste that was uniquely her.

That taste, something in him whispered, *that you will never escape, as long as you might live*.

But that was foolishness and Lao was no fool. Not even for this woman who made him want things for the first time.

Tonight, he intended to have them all.

He kissed her and he kissed her, angling his jaw to take more as he reached up and thrust his hand deep into the heavy, silken mass of her hair. He tugged until it all came free, falling down around them to cocoon them both in more scent, more heat.

Lao kept kissing her until he could feel her wriggling helplessly in his lap, telling him without words that she wanted him as much as he wanted her. He broke free of her mouth then, following the line of her neck.

He tasted his way across her delicate clavicle, then leaned back to he could slide his palms over the full curves of her breasts.

And gave himself over to the glory of this moment.

The glory of Chloe with her head thrown back, her eyes closed, as the candlelight danced over her face.

The sheer, sweet perfection of Chloe arching her back so that he could take more of her breasts in his hands—pressing herself into him with an intoxicating abandon that swept over him and through him like the strong spirits he rarely allowed himself.

And if she'd been any other woman, he would have cut to the chase, pulling her across his lap to straddle him so he could work his way between her thighs, then sink himself home.

But she was not any woman. She was his wife.

And more, Lao was quite certain that if Chloe had any experience at all, it was scant indeed.

When she whispered his name, he stood them both up, though it made him ache. Still, he put her on her feet and brushed her hair back from her face, and found it harder than it should have been not to get lost in her dark gaze. The heat there. The need all over her face that matched the same need in him.

"Come," he murmured, extending his hand.

Then waited for the heat and fire in her gaze to clear, just enough, so that when she laced her fingers with his, they both knew she meant it.

For a moment, there in the candlelight, there was only the sound of her breath, the steady beat of his heart, and the simmering heat where their hands were clasped together.

For a moment, and perhaps another, Lao simply let the heat between them swell.

But when he couldn't take any more of it he pulled her close, swung her up into his arms, and then strode with her to the spiral stair in the back of the tower that wound down to the room that waited for them.

"The magic goes on and on," Chloe whispered as he carried her into the small tower room that was done up with simple lushness. A fire in the grate to ward off the cold mountain air. A bed of iron, there against one stone wall. Piled high with soft linens and overstuffed mattresses for their ease and soft rugs on the floor to soothe away the chill of the stone.

"You have no idea," Lao told her, laying her out gently on the bed and following her down into the mattresses' soft embrace. "This is only the beginning."

And then he showed her what he meant.

He luxuriated in the fact that he could spread out with her at last, stretching along the length of her body so he could explore her in full.

All of her. Finally.

Lao shrugged his way out of his clothes as they got in his way and the barrier of linen and cloth became too much. And he stripped Chloe, too, with far more care.

Until she lay before him in nothing but a scant bit of lace between her thighs.

"You have not done this before," he said as he crawled over her, having finally dispensed with his clothing entirely. Her chest was moving, her breath coming in hard pants, and her eyes were big.

But she was flushed.

Everywhere.

She opened her mouth as if to speak, but no words came out. Instead, she pressed her lips together, then shook her head. Side to side, as if in distress.

"I'm sorry," she whispered.

Lao settled in beside her, returning his attention to her perfect breasts. To the proud nipples that stood high, begging for his mouth.

He obliged. One, then the other.

"Why would you apologize?" he murmured against her flesh.

She was arching up against him, pressing her nipple into his mouth, letting out a kind of sigh he thought might play like a symphony in his head forever.

"Everyone knows you must have had a million lovers," she managed to say, though her voice was broken now. "There's no possible way I can live up to any of them."

"The only thing you need to concern yourself with is this," he told her. He waited until she looked at him, her eyes so dark they seemed nearly black. And wildly glossy. "With me. Whatever happens here, between us. There is nothing else, *dusci mia*."

"But—"

"I will need you to say it, Chloe."

Though he didn't think she would, for a breath. Then one more.

Then, "You," she said softly. "Me. And nothing else, Lao."

He made a low sound of approval, then withdrew from her breasts so he could make his way down the length of her body.

And he remembered that beach in Brazil too well, so he glutted himself on the indentation of her waist, the rounded jut of her hips. He lost himself in circles around her navel, making her moan and shift against him.

Then, at last, he made his way down to that scrap of lace she wore. And while she bucked her hips against him, he wrapped his hands around her, holding her where he wanted her as he played. He used his mouth to taste her, finding his way to the softest part of her and sucking her in, fabric and all.

She made a broken sound and strained against him. And the sounds she made seemed to break something in him, too.

Lao helped himself to the glory she offered him, quickly stripping the lace off of her hips, down her legs, then tossing it aside. Then, finally, he settled himself between her legs, lifting her bottom into his hands so he could lick his way into her softness.

And then, once again, he feasted on the banquet of her.

He brought her to the edge, let her dance there, then pulled back.

It was not until her hands were sunk deep in

his hair and she was sobbing out his name so that it echoed off the wall and came back at them. It was not until her heels drummed against his back that he threw her over, letting her buck and writhe beneath his mouth.

Then he only started all over again.

And Lao had waited for this moment. He had wanted her for far too long, so now that he had her, he took his time.

And when she had shattered again and again, and was making soft little noises in the back of her throat, he crawled up the length of her body once more. He gathered her beneath him, gritting his teeth at how easily she came to him. How she wrapped her arms around his neck and gazed up at him. Maybe even *into* him.

Only then did he notch himself between her thighs, ease himself into her softness, and then—without waiting any longer or giving her a chance to tense—thrust deep.

Chloe sucked in a ragged breath, the eyes she'd let fall shut flying open.

And Lao held himself still, watching in a kind of wonder as she let out a long, slow breath that he could feel ripple all through her body.

Which meant all through his, too.

She began to experiment on her own, moving her hips against his. As if testing his length, his depth.

And he let her, doing nothing at all except holding himself there above her. She grew bolder. She began to lift her hips to take as much of him as possible, then dragged herself back, slowly.

On and on she went, concentrating on what she did with a ferocity and focus that made Lao's mouth water. So he let her do as she liked. He let her play with this, with him, finding what she needed, and working her way toward that bliss.

Her intensity made him feel something like humbled.

But she couldn't quite get there, and he waited, the muscles in his arms beginning to shake—and not from the exertion—as he let her figure that out on her own.

"Please," she whispered, and it was the prettiest sound he'd ever heard. "Please, Lao."

So he took pity on her, at last.

And then he took control.

He took her wrists in one hand, hauling them up and over her head so her back arched once more and her breasts danced as he thrust into her.

Lao went deep. And hard enough to make her moan as he took her past where she'd reached on her own and straight on into the sweet heat only he could make for her.

For them.

He set a demanding pace and felt an enormous

wildfire lick its way all over his body when she met it. Exulted in it.

Cried out his name like it was a song.

And this time, when she shattered, he lost himself right along with her, secure in the knowledge that he had gotten exactly what he wanted.

That he had broken the spell she had over him.

At last.

CHAPTER SIX

THEIR WEDDING NIGHT might have been five years late, but for Chloe, it was worth the wait.

More than worth it.

Because finally—*finally*—she'd gotten everything she'd ever dreamed of, and more, from her remote, forbidding former stepbrother. Everything she had pretended she didn't want in the light of day. Everything she'd pretended she didn't crave, when deep down, she'd always known better.

He taught her things she hadn't even known were possible.

She had never considered herself *truly* married these last five years. But she also knew she was, in fact, married. And maybe that was why she hadn't been in any great rush to experiment with the boundaries of their in-name-only arrangement.

Then again, maybe the mantle of his protection had been the perfect excuse to keep herself from succumbing to the urge to do something about her innocence with any of the uninspiring boys who were always hanging around her group of friends.

Lao was no boy. He was *man*, and she had learned that with every touch, every scrape of tongue and hint of teeth. She had understood the entire purpose of her body at last, when he'd showed her what they could do with it. What they could feel, together.

She would have said that she preferred all the bare-chested, hairless men she'd seen so many pictures of over the years, but it was only when she was tangled up in Lao, her face buried in the places where his dusting of dark hair made everything *so much better*, that she got it.

That she more than got it. Some part of her wished she could live forever on that dancing edge of the world, lost in sensation and hurtling toward the next bright implosion, as close to Lao as it was possible to get—

She wished she could go back in time and have her wedding night five years ago, so they could have spent this time perfecting this new-to-her art at which Lao, clearly, was a maestro. She wished she could go even further back and assure the younger teenager with the unwieldly crush on her worldly, faintly disapproving stepbrother that it would all work out.

In the most glorious possible way.

Chloe hadn't held on to her virginity because it had mattered to her in any way. She hadn't consciously been waiting for Lao, for this. She hadn't let herself imagine anything like this could ever happen. But it was immediately apparent to her that she would have regretted wasting her time on some lesser man.

He took her again that night and he was there when she woke up the next morning, lying beside her with a gleaming approval in his dark gaze that quickly washed away any impulse she might have had to feel ashamed about the previous night's wild abandon.

Instead, she felt a little bit like the goddesses that had once roamed these Italian shores.

She imagined he might take her all over again. She longed for him to do exactly that, amazed anew that she could feel her body's demands so acutely—and that he clearly knew, without her needing to tell him.

She could see it in the way he didn't quite smile.

Instead, he set about putting her clothes back on her body rather than removing them. Dressing her like she was his very own creation. Even helping her into one shoe, then the next, in a manner that left her feeling shivery. And flushed from within.

Then he threw on his own clothes and did not seem to notice or care that, for once, he looked very nearly…rumpled. Not his normal immaculate self, the very definition of male sophistication.

It felt like intimacy.

Especially when Lao led her out of that tower and back up the path they had come down the night before. As if they were walking, together, into this new day. This new version of *them*.

Chloe was absurdly grateful for the hand he held, leading her along the path. Because she felt so changed. So altered from the woman who had boarded that plane outside of London only the day before.

And she couldn't tell if the fact she felt remade was what made the world sparkle as it did. Or if it was simply the beauty of the Sicilian morning, the ancient perfection of the Monteleone estate, rolling out before her as the man she hadn't dared dream about directly led her inside.

He took her back into the castle, but did not lead her to her own bedchamber. He led her instead into the bathroom suite that sprawled between her chamber and his. There, without a word spoken between them since she'd woken up to find him gazing at her, he set about stripping her of her clothes and his all over again.

When he was finished he lifted her into his arms, taking her to the great copper tub that stood watch over the fields far below. She thought to whisper something to him, some acknowledgment of what had passed between them—but didn't dare.

The expression on his face was too intense, his focus too fierce, as he set about washing her. Everywhere.

And when he had smoothed warm water and a soap that smelled of tangerine and woodsmoke all over her, even between her legs, he rinsed her with the handheld sprayer. Then he lifted her again and carried her, wet and slippery, to the distinctly modern shower stall that stood nearby.

He finally took her again there, his mouth against the nape of her neck, her hands braced against the tiled wall, her head tipped back to let her cries pour out.

Sometime later that morning, she'd woken in his bed to find him dressed to his usual standard of bespoke perfection and heading toward the door.

"Where are you going?" Chloe asked in a voice gone rough from all the crying and moaning she'd been doing. Even hearing it made her skin warm all over again.

"The commitments I have wait for no man, be he a Monteleone or not," Lao had replied. He had sounded the way he always did, darkly untroubled by the concerns of anything around him.

Chloe pushed herself up on one elbow, shoving the heavy weight of her hair out of her way. She had not meant to be particularly provocative, but she watched as his gaze fell to where her breast peeked over the covers she had pulled over her sometime earlier.

His steel-gray eyes gleamed a fine, bright silver, but he did not come to her.

"I am sure you can find something or other to amuse yourself here, Chloe," he said in that cool way of his. "Though I can't promise anything as rewarding as the odd press junket or art show."

It was only later, after she'd napped again— and deeper—that she realized there was an insult wrapped up in that.

But she was entirely too sated, her body as brand-new to her as if it was her very first day on the planet, to care.

Later that afternoon, her attendants found her again. She was lying near one of the inlaid pools that dotted the terraced garden levels along one sloping side of the mountain, meaning at any moment to crack open the book she'd brought with her. Something brightly covered and fun-looking that she certainly hadn't found in his musty old library of tomes. She'd brought it with her from her last trip to a Waterstones to see what her former colleagues were publishing and promoting these days.

But the memories of last night were too delicious, too stirring, *too much.*

"Come," the attendants urged her as they stood above her, beaming with that same good cheer. "The master wants an early meal this evening."

Chloe understood that meant that the preparation for the master's early dinner needed to get underway as soon as possible. And she found she rather liked the idea that she could let them turn her into a party favor.

Up in her bedchamber, it seemed like great fun to let them go through the wardrobe that had been assembled for her. They settled on a confection of a dress that floated all about her and made her feel like a princess. They even fastened a sort of tiara in her hair that made her sparkle with every step.

She had to remind herself, as she moved through the castle a little too eagerly later, that she was the one who had decided to throw herself into this. Meaning she could remove herself, too.

You're not being swept away, she told herself as she walked. *You are simply enjoying a swim.*

But then Lao took one look at her, ordered his staff out of the small salon where he had been waiting for her, and had her right there on the table.

As if she was a dessert he could not wait to sample.

And sweeter by far than the *sfincia* they had

much later, curled up together in one of the chairs near the fireplace in Lao's rooms.

Another day passed in the same dreamy manner, sex and sun and Chloe's delight in both her own body and his, but then it was Monday.

She woke up early. So early that Lao, who never seemed to rest, was still asleep in the bed beside her. He was golden and bold against the pale linens, his eyelashes much longer than they seemed when she could see all that steel and thunder in his gaze.

There was no reason that should tug at her heart, Chloe told herself sternly.

No reason whatsoever.

She slid out of the bed, then padded over to the great glass doors that opened up to one of the many balconies in this castle that brought the island inside. The sky above, the sea below, as if they were all part of each other. As if they were all the same thing.

And then she stood there, looking out, feeling a kind of aching deep inside her that already felt like loss.

"What troubles you, Chloe?" came Lao's voice from the bed behind her, though it was gravelly just then, as if he was deliberately aiming straight between her legs.

She smiled as she turned to face him. Lao did

not pull his curtains closed, so the dawning light was already making its way into the room to find him on the bed, all that golden skin dusted with dark black hair like a dream come true against the sheets. Her dream. Her truth.

Chloe didn't understand how it was she'd spent days now, memorizing every inch of him, and still her mouth watered for more.

Still she felt as if she could never, ever get enough.

"I'm sorry this has to end," she said softly.

And meant it far more than she intended to share with him. Because she might have been a bit *dozy*, sure, but she hoped she wasn't that much of a fool. She hoped she wasn't silly enough to pour out her heart to a man she'd spent the weekend with, even if it was Lao.

Especially because it was Lao.

It wasn't playing games. It was because intimacy and pleasure were a tangle inside her and yet the dark steel of his gaze was the same.

There was a thread of feminine wisdom deep within her that made it clear that some things were better kept to herself.

His dark brow rose in that way of his. It was a quiet display of arrogance so intense it should have been preposterous. But this was Lao. It was simply who he was.

"End?" he asked, as if she'd lapsed into some kind of gibberish. "Why on earth would anything end? I thought I was clear. I have no intention of divorcing you."

Chloe blinked. "But it's Monday." When he only gazed back at her without comprehension, she found herself almost sputtering. "I… I do have to go to work, Lao."

Another man might have thrown back his head and laughed. That wasn't Lao. But still, she could see by the way he shifted in the bed that she amused him. Deeply.

"You do not have to work." He shook his head as if the very notion baffled him. "You are a Monteleone, in both name and fact now. You are my wife. The only work I require from you will take place here. In this bed."

Something about that seemed jagged within her, like broken glass. Chloe wanted to argue, but he was crooking his finger at her.

And it was as good as throwing a rope around her and tugging her across the vast expanse of the room toward him. She moved without meaning to, making her way to the side of the bed where he hooked his arm around her and tumbled her down with him.

The he rolled her over and lit them both up all over again.

Much later that morning, she texted the gallery to let them know that she was taking a bit of a leave of absence, and couldn't really have said why it was that their dismissive reply—No problems, love. Drop in when you can—left her feeling… almost listless.

As if there was a truth here she didn't want to see.

"You matter," her father had told her once, in a voice as close to stern as Charlie Stapleton ever got. She had been a young girl then, trying to process the fact that her mother had traded her role as a parent for a small fortune and a house to go with it in a distant country. "The world is a better place with you in it, my girl. That's true no matter what your mother chooses to do. No matter what anyone tells you or wants you to believe. You matter, Chloe."

She had held on to that as a child, the way some children held on to a much-loved blanket. Later, when she had been a newly minted teenager, her stepmother had found her stomping around the garden on a cold December morning and had slipped into place beside her.

"A bit of a moody morning," Portia had said. "Just right for brooding about in the cold, I'd say."

Chloe hadn't had much use for her mother and hadn't heard from her in ages. But still, she'd thought that maybe she'd better put on a good show and resist her father's marriage to Portia, because that seemed the sort of thing a decent daughter would do.

That had lasted all of four seconds. Portia had been a force of nature in the best possible way, sweeping up everyone she encountered in her irrepressible good cheer.

"Everyone I know has a plan," Chloe had burst out. "Everyone I know at school is either planning a brilliant university career, already has a gap year lined up, or has plotted out their whole life. Where they want to move. What they want to do. Who they want to be. When all I can manage is being thirteen."

"All you need to be is Chloe," Portia had said in that matter-of-fact way she had, as if she expected the planets would align themselves behind her at her say so.

By then, Chloe had believed they would too.

"But I don't have any idea who that is!" Chloe had cried.

Next to her, Portia hadn't rushed to offer a solution. She had considered Chloe's outburst thoughtfully, as if it mattered to her as deeply as her own issues must, and that was one of the reasons why Chloe had loved her so much. She had always, always listened.

Losing that had been like losing a limb.

"I don't know why you think you should know," Portia had replied eventually, the cold December air making both of their faces pink.

It had made Chloe imagine they were the same. Or could be.

"It seems to me that a life is the process of finding that out. Just because everyone else appears to be on a schedule, with everything sorted, that doesn't mean you need to do the same. All you need to do—all you ever need to do—is what works for you."

And now, here on the same land in Sicily where Portia had once lived, Chloe wondered if she'd been waiting her whole life for this without even knowing it. Because she hadn't been particularly good at any of the things she'd tried, no matter how much she might like talking about art. But what became clear to her, and quickly, was that she was excellent at being this new, full version of Lao's wife.

Like I was born for it, she thought a bit smugly as one week rolled into the next, so that a month swept by and into the next before she noticed.

Because he could hardly keep his hands off her. She wasn't sure he tried. Her days were spent recovering and her nights were filled with Lao.

With learning all the different ways that they could make each other come apart.

Nothing was forbidden. Nothing was sacred.

They explored each other, chasing that explosiveness, that drugging release, that endless well of passion.

"I suppose this counts as the honeymoon," she said one evening, when they had both showed tremendous restraint and had made it all the way through dinner without tearing each other's clothes off. Now they sat in Lao's favorite salon in the main part of the castle, sipping at espresso to balance out the wine and the sweets while the stars outside gleamed down over the tangled slope of the mountainside. "Although perhaps not for you. Since you do insist on working all the time."

"Empires do not run themselves, *dusci mia.*"

And for fun, Chloe liked to catalog all the ways that Lao was different now. Now that their relationship had changed so much. Now that he was sharing his life with her. He was still Lao, of course. He was still *stern*, but she had a much different context for that now.

Because *stern* now made her shiver, then melt. And perhaps because of that, he seemed less stern to her outside of bed, even unbending enough to lounge there across from her as he was now. As if he knew how to relax.

"What exactly is your empire?" she asked idly, when really, she was congratulating herself on not launching herself at him the way she wanted to. "I read a whole article about the Monteleone family a few years ago. If anything, it managed to make you and your history seem that much more mysterious."

"There's a lesson there, I should think. You'd be much better off not believing what you read."

"I was surprised there was any article at all, if I'm honest. I thought you were opposed to publicity in all its forms. As ancient Monteleone family policy."

"I am." He took a sip, then held the espresso cup in his palm in a manner that sent that same delirious heat dancing all through her body. And when he looked up, there was a considering sort of expression on his face, though he was aiming it out the window and further down the mountainside. "I was taught when I was very young to abhor the kind of flashiness and attention-seeking that so many aspire to these days. Yet at the same time, if we never allow anyone near us at all, we risk creating a sense of mystery that some find irresistible. This has played out in a thousand regrettable ways over the years."

She wanted to ask him how, but didn't. Because she had a sense he not only wouldn't answer, but might even have forgotten he was telling her these things. And Chloe did not want him to stop.

"It has always been my goal to make those who wish to solve the mystery, such as it is, of the Monteleone family feel as if they've already solved it. Hence, articles that pretend to expose me and my history, but these are never truly exposing. In the kind of circles that I run, less is always more and vulnerabilities are only ever seen as weapons to be used against whoever is so unwary as to show their bellies."

She found herself frowning at her own espresso, wondering if it was the rich brew that made her heart beat so fast. "You make it sound like some kind of game, to hide in plain sight."

"It is easy enough." He lifted his shoulder. "For one thing, I do not attend the sort of social events that end up in the papers in the first place. We live in an age where people believe existence only occurs if it is recorded and then disseminated. It is not so much that I try to be invisible but that I simply don't take part in the endless internet celebrity hustle. Monteleones existed long before there was any such thing and they will endure long after, too. If I have an empire, that is what it is. The knowledge of time, how it passes, and what is required of me to make sure my family continues on."

Chloe had no idea why that seemed to poke at

her. As if he was insulting her, when he wasn't. "The internet is the new town square. It's how people communicate, like it or not."

"But we are not now seated in a town square, are we? We are at the top of a mountain, in a very old castle, overlooking an even more ancient island. My ancestors retreated from town squares generations ago. I don't participate in the kind of communication most people do. I allow people to find me or I don't."

His arrogance really should have knocked her out of her chair. She thought she really ought to despair of herself for finding it, instead, attractive. Her body was already clamoring for him—and the more arrogant he was, the more she seemed to want him.

Maybe she was broken.

Though…she didn't *feel* broken. She felt hungry.

"You can be looked up on the internet the same as anyone else, Lao," she said, frowning at him as if that might make all that hunger go away when, by now, she knew better. There was only one fix, and it was glorious, but it only made her hungrier. "You're not a ghost, no matter how you might wish you were."

"I control it," he said in that voice of quiet thunder that she felt as much as she heard. "That would not be possible to do if I allowed myself to become tabloid fodder. I control when I am mentioned, and by whom. And in so doing, not only control *how* I am discussed, but who takes part in the discussion." He regarded her then, a faintly curious look on his face. "Why does this subject interest you?"

And she wanted to tell him something lofty and analytical, something that would make her seem more on his level than some dreamy child bride he'd had to rescue more than once already. It astonished her, how deeply she wanted that.

"Because I don't want to be a ghost," she heard herself say instead, without realizing those words were on her tongue. But she'd said them, hadn't she? And now they hung in the air and couldn't be taken back, no matter how high his brow arched. "And I...don't want to have children who disappear in plain sight."

She hadn't told him about her birth control situation. He hadn't asked. There was something in that, too, that she supposed she ought to look at. That he had simply made pronouncements, then taken her to his bed, and clearly had every intention of fulfilling his own wishes as he saw fit.

Whether she had explicitly agreed or not.

Then again, she knew without having to ask that he would not take it well that she'd chosen not to share the fact she'd had that shot. And that in not telling him, she was deceiving him—especially when she mentioned children. Chloe liked to tell herself that was the reason why she didn't pursue these little threads of concern and disquiet that cropped up inside her, now and again.

But she didn't take this opportunity to correct the situation.

Lao was setting aside his espresso and rising to his feet. Once he did, he reached for her, pulling her to him and then hauling her up into his arms.

"The ghost life has much to recommend it," he told her, and she wanted to think that he was joking. But the truth was, she couldn't tell. There was too much behind those eyes of his, but he never shared it. "Let me show you."

And he did. This time he backed her up against the nearest ancient wall, without any kind of finesse. It was hard, deep, and wildly intense.

It was magic.

Because she was always ready for him, now. Because she wanted him more by the second. It only took him tossing her skirts up, holding her as he worked his zipper, then slamming himself home.

It was that easy. It was that *perfect*.

She had taken to biting down on his neck she rode out her pleasure, as if there was something in the quick violence of it that made her shake apart even more.

Or as if, something in her whispered as she panted in the aftermath, *you want to carry his taste on your tongue—the more intense, the better.*

Another night, weeks later, they walked outside after their evening meal. They took in the warm air and the lingering light, as summer waxed on all around them.

"I think of your mother here," she said, looking toward the riotous expanse of rose bushes that reminded her of the flowers Portia had tended so lovingly on her father's estate in England. "She must have loved how the gardens grow in this climate."

But Lao did not respond. His jaw seemed to harden as he looked off, down the mountainside the way he did too often.

"Your mother was no ghost," Chloe pointed out, because those jagged things inside her never went anywhere. They only waited for her to get fed up with the poking. "Of all the things someone might say to describe Portia, the word *ghost* would never come up."

Lao turned that dark look on her, and her breath caught, for there was something forbidding there. Something she would heed, if she were wise. "Still holding on to that conversation, are you? When I thought I taught you there are a thousand glorious ways to haunt this place, at the least."

Apparently Chloe was not wise, for she pushed on. "You said that was my role. And she was the only other Monteleone wife I ever knew." She let out a laugh, thinking of her stepmother and her many projects, from her roses to her stepdaughter to her numerous charities. "I doubt very much that she sat about all day, without any kind of purpose, waiting for your father's notice."

Lao stopped walking. "You did not know my mother as a Monteleone wife, Chloe. You knew her only as a Monteleone widow. They are not the same." And before Chloe could respond to that, much less the darkness in his voice and all over his face, as if he wanted to drown out the early stars and what remained of the summer light, he went on. "And you are mistaken. My father had extremely old-fashioned ideas about her role here. She was to oversee the various tutors he selected for the education he expected me to have here, before I went off to boarding school. She managed the house and the staff, but always according to his demands. She was otherwise expected to be available to him, silent unless spoken to, and charming to any guests." Something ugly seemed to pulse there, deep in the thunder she could see in his gaze, but he only pressed his lips together until it passed.

"You, Chloe, already possess a greater degree of freedom than my mother ever did"

"That sounds hideous." Chloe's voice was low, but that didn't hide the hurt in it. Though whether she hurt for Portia or herself, she was ashamed to discover she couldn't say. "I can't imagine your mother locked away like that." She swallowed, hard, but Lao only gazed down at her in that affronted manner of his that made everything inside her...shudder. "She was so...vibrant. Alive. Why would anyone want to lock her up?"

"For precisely those reasons. Because Monteleones do not call attention to themselves." Lao looked back at the castle. "This was only a ruin, then. We lived down at the manor house on a lower part of the mountain."

"I've never seen it."

But she knew. She knew that this was what his eyes searched for in the dark, down that slope, again and again. She knew this was a huge part of the secrets he kept locked away inside of him. She *knew*.

"That is because I had it torn down," Lao told her, confirming what she knew already. And there was something in his voice, then. It made a prickling thing wind its way down the length of Chloe's spine. "This castle was where my mother liked to come when she wished to be alone. And be herself.

Once my father died, I decided that I might as well reclaim its place as the family seat."

She felt the strangest rush of emotion tear through her, then. It was how stiffly he stood there before her. It was how little he said, and yet how much there was stuffed in all around the careful words, telling her far more. It was the way he frowned out across the darkness, always in the same direction.

"Lao," she whispered. "What exactly did your father do to your mother?"

It seemed to take him much too long to look back at her. And when he did, there was no hint of that frown. That darkness.

She could see nothing on his face but that same desire that marked them both.

"Lao—" she tried again.

"Enough talking," he growled, and then jerked her into his arms.

And she knew that there was something here. That she should fight. That she should protest, at the very least.

But his kiss was too marvelous. He knew her body too well. She was on fire within seconds, and then entirely wanton in his arms, right there in the dirt where the roses grew.

And it was not until a few days later, after she'd tried repeatedly to return to the topic of his torn-down manor house and his parents' relationship, that she realized there was a pattern here.

Lao didn't want to talk to her about anything of substance. He always changed the subject, and always in the same way. Very much as if what he wanted from her was the same thing his own father had wanted from a wife. Hadn't he told her so, more or less, already?

Sexual availability and obedience. And instead of one child, who could likely be managed easily enough and then sent off to school, Lao wanted four. She doubted that was an accident.

She doubted any of this was an accident. And he hadn't said that having so many children would give her something to do, but once she got that thought in her head she couldn't seem to get rid of it.

Good job you're on the shot, she congratulated herself heartily. *And that you kept that to yourself all this time.*

It was already August when he flew off for meeting somewhere else, leaving her for the first time since she'd come here at the end of May. She thought if she was someone else, she could put the time she was alone here to good use. She would... investigate him, somehow. Round up the staff, ask them questions, and take over the whole place. But she didn't.

Because they had all made it clear in a thousand small ways that they were entirely loyal to Lao. She took long walks around the property instead, heading out farther than the gardens. With him gone she had no one to answer to, so she wasted little time in finding an overgrown but clear path down the side of the mountain, heading straight toward that place where Lao's eyes were always drawn.

The path ended in a field, but she saw it from the path down and knew it for what it was—an overgrown footprint of the house that had once stood here.

It was a warm day, but she shivered. The house had been set on a flat expanse on the slope, the mountain and the castle up above with the better part of Sicily far below.

She stood there in the forgotten rooms, where grass now grew and vines tangled this way and that, trying to imagine what it must have been like to grow up here. Suspended between the sky and the sea and a mother and father who could be called, at best, harsh.

Chloe spent an afternoon there, as if the way the breeze whipped at her was some kind of evidence. As if the way the sun beat down with the birds singing could unlock the secrets of Lao Monteleone.

As if the way her heart ached for him could save

them both from these ghosts she was beginning to believe were monsters.

The next day, when he returned, she told herself she would wait to be summoned. But she couldn't hold to it. She heard the car pull up out front and couldn't keep herself from racing down the stairs to meet him.

"I like this eagerness," he told her in that dark way of his, pulling her up against him, giving her a hard kiss.

Then he was tugging her along with him, back up the stairs and into his bedroom. He tossed her down on the bed, making up for those days they'd spent apart.

Making sure she hadn't forgotten him. Or this.

He didn't tell her where he'd been. He didn't tell her what sort of meetings he had to take. She didn't ask.

And it was hard to tell if she was playing along, or if she didn't quite dare.

Later, Lao had food brought to the room. They sat together, wrapped up in the softest robes, out on that balcony as the day's heat rose around them until the breeze rushed in to wash it away.

"I found your old house," she said, and watched him as she said it.

Because maybe she did dare, after all.

He didn't move. He didn't even look at her, and

yet she could feel the chill, the dark, the hint of far-off thunder.

Then Lao turned to her—but there was nothing on his face. No frown. No disapproval. Just that hot, gleaming steel.

"That must have been a pretty spot to live in," she said, and she knew she was pushing him, she *wanted* to push him, and maybe she *needed* it—

Chloe caught her breath as he reached for her, but it was only to lift her from her seat and pull her over his lap.

Then his mouth was on hers, hot and demanding. His hands moved between them, arranging her body so she could straddle him and he could surge deep inside of her with one sure stroke.

And she didn't forget as he slammed his way in. She didn't forget as he lit them both on fire, letting that particular storm of theirs in again. And again.

She didn't forget as he took her tight nipples in his mouth, ratcheting up that sensation to near unbearable heights.

She didn't forget as he reached between them, finding the proud center of her need, and pinching it until she sobbed out her pleasure.

Not when she shattered that first time, or a time or two again for good measure.

Not even when he carried her inside and sank into that tub with her, holding her before him with her back to his front and kissing away the words any time she tried to speak.

She didn't forget, but to be certain, Chloe tried again and again over the next week or so. Until there was no denying that it was true.

Her husband wanted very specific things from her. Her body yes. Again and again and again. But when it came to conversation, he wanted it light, on the surface, and easy. Or he was happy enough with silence.

This man who had been the defining force in her life for as long as she could remember, so long that the fact she was in love with him had been as unworthy of direct mention as the existence of the sky above, didn't love her back. His kindness had, perhaps, not been quite so kind after all.

Because all he wanted from her was sex. Perhaps an heir—or four.

But what he didn't want was Chloe. Not the reality of Chloe, the whole person who existed outside their bed and the white-hot fire of what they did to each other when they were naked.

And she wasn't sure that she could bear it. Not if he didn't see *her* when she looked at him. Not if the only man she'd ever loved, the man she'd dreamed about almost the whole of her life, didn't think she mattered beyond the children he wanted her to give him or the life he wanted her to live, entirely on his terms.

Not if the only way she could have him was to make herself another one of his ghosts.

CHAPTER SEVEN

"I'VE BEEN RESEARCHING the roses," Chloe announced at dinner one night.

"Have you?"

Lao considered her over his glass of wine. She sat, flushed and pretty, in the chair opposite him. The prettiness was a genetic gift, he knew, but he'd had a hand in that flush. He had decided that he fancied an *aperitivo* this evening and had found his way into her dressing room earlier, scattering her attendants with a tilt of his head. Chloe had been dressed in nothing but a strapless bra and matching bit of lace panties, a confection in human form.

She had made him feel drunk when he did not allow himself drunkenness.

He had knelt down before her, drawn one silky smooth leg over his shoulder, and drank his fill.

And then, to prove to himself that he was under no kind of spell, he had not taken his own pleasure in her.

Because he could wait, he had assured himself. He *kept* assuring himself. This was not about need. This was about the future he intended make happen with this woman. Not just any woman—his wife.

And that did not require his own release.

The results of his handiwork were before him now. All that glossy need in her gaze. All that heat in her cheeks that he knew reached every last part of her lush little body.

He had checked.

"I looked online, of course, but in your library too," she said. After clearing her throat and squirming in her seat. She looked edible—though he could see she meant to sound serious. "I can't find the specific variety of rose that grows here anywhere."

Lao did not precisely sigh. He sat back in his seat and considered her. "What I can't help but notice is that you seem determined to find a mystery here, no matter where it is you look. I am tempted to find this insulting. Perhaps you may have heard it said that a rose is…just a rose, Chloe. Sometimes they grow wild and mean nothing at all."

Her eyes flashed a bit at that but she didn't comment directly. She never did. He had never told her that she must keep any hint of her temper to herself, the way he could distinctly recall his own father lecturing Portia back in the day.

"Your silence must be gracious, woman," his father had thundered. "You must reflect the Monteleone legacy with every glance, every word, every expression on your face. What you think, what you feel—these things matter not at all."

Lao had never said such things to his wife.

Still, though he knew that he'd seen that flash in her gaze, she spoke instead of the damned roses. "I hunted down your gardener. He does not have any English so I had one of the women who help with my dressing translate for me. But he agreed. It's a different sort of rose, Lao."

And a man who was not under this woman's spell might have laughed at that, because it was so obvious where she was heading. But Lao had never been much given to laughter, so he only sighed. "Stop dancing around whatever it is you wish to say to me, please. Simply say it, Chloe, so that we might eat our meal in peace."

There was no disguising the temper in her gaze, then. She looked nothing short of mutinous, and he told himself it was the reaction of a child—but try as he might, he could not truly think of her as a child. Oh, he would like to. It would suit him only too well to dismiss her as immature in every way.

But there was no doubt whatsoever that he had a woman in his bed, not a girl.

Lao could not quite bring himself to lie about that. Not even in the privacy of his own head.

Chloe did not glare at him. Not quite. "Your gardener and I agreed that these roses must have been cultivated. I think your mother made her own variety here."

And then she looked at him as if there were some significance in that. Some lesson that he should take to heart.

What a pity he did not have one.

"My mother was an avid gardener," he said offhandedly. Agreeably enough. "If I recall correctly, she maintained that a house was no home without roses set to bloom and planted them accordingly wherever she happened to find herself."

There was something about the way Chloe studied him, then. As if she was far shrewder than he liked to give her credit for and could see much more than he thought. A notion he did not choose to entertain. "But she did not live in the castle. You said she lived in the manor house, didn't you? That you all did, until your father died."

"My mother did her duty." Lao was uncomfortably aware that his voice was bordering on... tense. "She lived in the manor house until my father's death. Then she moved into one of the guest cottages. It made the decision to renovate the castle easy."

"What about the decision to raze the manor house?" Chloe asked.

Perhaps a touch too sweetly, as he considered it.

And as it happened, he found himself craving dessert. He reached across the table and took the wineglass she held from her hand. Then he pulled her up and into his arms, drinking in the little sighing sound she made, the little hitch in the back of her throat. The noises he found himself thinking about far too often when his attention should have been focused on more important things. The noises he was beginning to think might haunt him for the rest of his life.

"I thought we were speaking of roses," he said, his mouth against her neck, letting his teeth graze the tender flesh he found there until she shuddered and broke out in goose bumps. The way he knew she would.

He chased her words and her mysteries and her canny questions away with the heat of his mouth, hauling her up against him, his hands already busy. He reached beneath her skirts, happy that she rarely bothered with panties any longer, and certainly wasn't wearing any tonight.

Lao had removed them himself upstairs.

Maybe he had known that he would need her

in a fury, like this, angling her back onto the table and pounding into her, his thrusts so deep and so true that she was not the only one who shuddered.

She was not the only one who seemed ravaged by this unbearable heat between them.

But the only thing Lao cared about any longer was when she shattered in his arms, his name on her lips.

Like every night, he set her to rights when their breathing slowed again. He tucked himself away. Then he carried her upstairs to the bedchamber he had never intended to share with anyone and started it all over again, from scratch.

In the mornings, he rose as if he had not been up all night, desperate for her in the dark. He readied himself for work and put in his usual long hours of endless calls and meetings, tending to the only garden he had been taught to care about.

This ever-growing, ever-shifting Monteleone legacy, with its tendrils like vines, reaching this way and that. In his mind's eye it seemed to him that the influence of his name alone wrapped up the whole globe and held it tight.

Just as the legacy itself held him in the same way.

He sat in the office he'd built himself so he could always look not only at the sweep of Sicily and the world beyond, but the remains of the manor house below him. Every day, with only a steep cliff and too much history before him, he could comfort himself with the knowledge that this was only temporary.

Only and ever temporary, this summer. It would be fall before he knew it.

It always was.

This madness, this sensual hurricane, had already gone on longer than any of the affairs he'd ever participated in his adult life. His lovers had always been sophisticated women in possession of their own fortunes, with appropriately excellent pedigrees, so that, should news of their union get out somehow, it would raise no eyebrows. They had been universally overawed by him. Lao had chosen them carefully and pursued them quietly, and because of that, had always wondered why it was impossible to maintain any level of heat or interest much past the first month.

He could admit that it had been something of a relief to take those vows five years ago, and then demand of his own body that he ignore its own demands, his own needs, because above all else he was a man who did not break the promises he made.

And that was the explanation for his reaction to Chloe. He had spent time telling himself this. Because it had been years. He had been pent-up in a manner that he never had been before. It was no wonder that he had confused that for some particular, unique spell that Chloe had cast on him.

It was no wonder that those first two months had been a pageant of blistering need and that undying desire for her.

He told himself that, now, what animated him was this driving need to see her pregnant. To get the issue of his heir sorted, so he could step back. So he could put this steamy summer behind him.

"You must take care with women," his father had barked at him. The old man had already been in the first flush of his illness, though no one would know it for years yet.

"I always take care, Father," Lao had replied, trying not to show that he was offended. Because he had been just out of university and the last thing he could imagine wanting was the trouble of a child.

Unless it was a woman who might make demands on him outside his bed.

"I'm not speaking of sex," his father had bitten out at him in his usual cold manner. "I should hope you are not so cringingly stupid as to foist one of your bastards on the world. Because I promise you, Stanislao, should that happen, I will cut the both of you off and sire a new heir by morning."

Lao did not doubt that at all. Not for one moment. As far as he had ever been able to tell, his father was motivated by three things only.

Spite and money.

And, of course, the power that followed from each.

"I am very careful," he had replied. Stiffly.

His father had sat there in that oppressive study in the manor house, his heavy brows clapped together as he regarded his son. "What I am speaking of is the woman you will marry. And do not act as if you are unaware that you must marry to maintain the line."

That, too, was a deliberate slap. "I am aware of my duties."

His father had made a low noise, as if he had some doubts on that score. "I will tell you now, it will be a difficult choice. There are certain expectations of a Monteleone wife. She must be without peer. Her beauty must be a fact, not a debate. She must exude an old-world elegance without tipping too far over into that inbreeding that makes for horse faces and weak chins. Find a decently bred woman who other men might covet, but only if they possess enough sophistication to recognize her for the jewel she is."

Lao had nodded dutifully, while hoping he was not about to be sent off on a hunt for said jewel.

"I had no idea that you held my mother in such high regard."

"Your mother is a cautionary tale," his father had barked, and had gone a bit red in the face as he'd leaned forward, jabbing one of the cigars he loved to smoke in Lao's direction. "She commands far too much attention. She has a magnetism that has always offended me and should offend you, too, my boy. Because it is never a single personality that should claim the spotlight, but the Monteleone name."

Always the name. Always the family legacy.

As if he could hear his son's less-than-honorable thoughts, his father had growled and continued, "It is always the name, Lao. Never the man. And certainly never that man's wife. If you do not choose wisely, you will live out your days in turmoil. And I do not mean the wild sort of passion young men might find intriguing." His gaze had been cold. Bracing. "I mean war."

War, Lao had thought then—and thought now, too—was not the least bit appealing.

He found himself standing at those grand windows in his office on another summer morning, awash in another sensual hangover. He scowled out down the mountainside, past the field where the manor house had once stood. The only thing that remained in that field, off to one side and down the cliff some distance, was his father's grave. Lao liked to stand here, high above it, and remind himself that whatever else he might gain in this life, he too was destined for a lonely grave on a mountainside where only the family name mattered.

Before Chloe had come back, he had found that notion a comfort.

It had been much easier when he'd thought he knew exactly how things would go with the girl he'd married.

What he hadn't been prepared for on any level was that that lost, dreamy creature was entirely different when she was infused with the kind of confidence that came with regular, and regularly excellent, sex. Or a passion that he could not pretend, in the midst of it or outside of it, did not wreck him as it wrecked her.

He supposed that would give anyone an elevated sense of themselves.

It wasn't that he wished to crush it. He didn't.

But he could not encourage it, either.

Because his father had been difficult in a great many ways, but when it came to the care and protection of the Monteleone name, he had been right. Like it or not, he had always been right.

Lao knew that he could not afford to let his marriage take precedence over the Monteleone legacy. Especially when he had yet to make any inroads into the continuation of that legacy into the next generation.

But until he secured the line, he also could not dismiss his wife.

That the latter happened to align with his actual, personal desires only made him more suspicious of himself.

"It can't have been easy to grow up here, all alone," Chloe said another evening when they were walking outside in the garden. The scent of summer flowers perfumed the night air, the castle gleamed like a beacon up the hill from them, and Lao could pretend that he was civilized. Simply because he had not yet knocked her to the dirt and found his way between her thighs.

He told himself there were more and more of these moments, where he reacquainted himself with his self-control. And that they meant her hold on him was diminishing.

"I don't know what you mean," he managed to say with some semblance of good grace. "It is, as you can see very well, a true paradise. I had no complaints."

"You must have been very lonely."

"A Monteleone is never lonely," Lao replied mildly enough, intoning the words he had heard his father say a thousand times. "For he is forever surrounded by the deeds of his ancestors."

And he did not understand it when she laughed, then sobered quickly in response to whatever look he wore on his face.

"You're supposed to play as a child," she argued softly. "Not parrot back strange quotations about family lines. It sounds a bit creepy, don't you think?"

He stared down at her. "No, Chloe. I do not think."

"I told you." And there was a different sort of tension in her voice then. "I don't want to raise my children with ghosts. And I certainly don't want them to *become* ghosts."

That had struck Lao like a blow. "I am no ghost, if that is what you mean."

"If you say so" was her unsatisfactory reply.

And she was the one who lurched forward then, pressing her lips to his. Igniting that wildfire that always raged between them.

Lao responded the way he always did, though he knew she had done it to forestall whatever he'd been about to say.

It did not sit easy in him, that she should use his own best weapons against him. But he did not push her away, either.

Much later that night—after they had ravaged each other in the bed he did not even pretend they did not share, though they both knew that, supposedly, she had her own—he lay awake. He stared up at what remained of the ancient ceiling, reinforced with the steel girders that helped him remember that he must be the future no matter how steeped he was in the past.

That he had a duty to perform. That he knew all the appropriate steps to take, laid out carefully by all his ancestors.

What he could not do was allow the cancer of emotion to destroy him. Because he already knew where that went.

They had buried his father with very little pomp or circumstance, as befitted a man who had always preferred the shadows to the light. His mother had walked away first and Lao had let her go, thinking that she needed some time to herself, perhaps some space for what he assumed must be an even more complicated grief than the one he had been experiencing.

He did not know how long he stood there. But he remembered the very instant he'd smelled smoke.

The rest of it was a blur. The smoke, the flames. That he had fought to get the fire out, working with members of his staff as if they had all transformed themselves into firemen overnight. And when they'd finally got the fire out, and had lost relatively little in the process—only, he could not help but note, the master bedroom and the wing in which it had stood—he had found his mother wrapped in a blanket, staring sightlessly off toward the sea.

"Did you love him so much then?" Lao had asked her, not sure what that terrible weight was inside him, but assuming it must be more of that same unknowable grief. "That you can think of nothing but following him into the afterlife?"

This despite the war he had always known his parents waged between themselves. The war he had witnessed long before his father had called it such.

"Oh," Portia had said, sounding nothing like her vibrant self, "I loved him once. He knew that, and he used it against me in every possible way. Just as he used my love for you against me. Just as he used anything and everything I loved against me, so he could be sure that the only thing I could ever depend upon was him, for good or ill."

"Mother..." he had tried to say.

But she had looked at him with a kind of fractured, hard-earned wisdom in her gaze that he did not like to think about, even now.

"I walked into that house a silly-headed bride who hoped against hope that I would have a happy life, and your father disabused me of that foolish notion as quickly as possible. And then he made me live in it for near on twenty-five years. And

I find that I would rather sleep beneath the rose-bushes, thorns and all, up at the castle than spend one more night in this accursed house that was never, ever a home."

Lao thought of that, and it kept him awake.

In the morning, he meant to take himself off to work as usual, but Chloe was stirring. She smiled at him, her eyes sleepy and her body so warm, and then she sang in the shower.

And he was only a man.

He was only a man, and perhaps not much of one, because he followed her into all that steam and heat and made them both groan their way into the morning, not once, but twice.

When they'd finished, boneless and clinging to each other as the water poured down, he wrapped her up so carefully, squeezing out the water from her hair and binding it up the towel. Then he caught himself looking at her as if she was something far more than merely a puzzle he needed to crack.

And she smiled as if she couldn't help it.

"You look as if you've gone a little silly there, *dusci mia*," he said, though he knew he shouldn't. Because he knew better.

He knew better, and especially when her smile only widened.

"The silliest," she agreed, and then she sighed, a

big sound that seemed to well up from the deepest part of her. "Lao. I don't know how to say this…"

"Then do not feel you must," he replied sternly, because surely he had some premonition.

But she moved toward him, slid her arms around him, and smiled up at him as if he had placed the stars in their firmament.

And he was only a man, despite his father's best attempts to beat that out of him, and so he basked in it. He couldn't help himself.

He hated that he couldn't bear to step away… but he didn't.

"I love you," she whispered. "I don't know if that's allowed, but I do. I… I think maybe I always have?"

And he could not allow that.

He could not allow *love*.

No matter how his pulse became a drum, how he felt a terrible weight again that he thought he recognized, a vicious grief—

But he had always known his duty. Always.

So he looked down at her as if he pitied her. He told himself he did, and so he tapped her on the nose as he remembered doing, once long ago.

To remind them both of who they were.

"I need heirs, Chloe," Lao said coldly. "Not love poems. Let's remember who we are."

CHAPTER EIGHT

KNOWING SHE NEEDED to leave Lao was one thing.

Doing it was another.

Especially because, her broken heart notwithstanding, Chloe kept thinking that if she just tried a little bit harder, he would change his mind.

If she just kept at it, he would love her.

It was not lost on her that this was a very similar line of thought to the one she'd been swamped in years ago, when she was a little girl trying to make sense of her mother's defection. Somehow Chloe had come to the conclusion that Bianca Stapleton, always the center of her very own spotlight, was driven away by the child she'd always ignored.

That was the reason her father had given her that little talk about *mattering*.

"The truth is, my darling," he had told Chloe when she was older, "Bianca never loved a thing on this earth but herself and I doubt she ever will."

It was Portia who had loved Chloe, as if Chloe

was hers. It was Portia who had raised her in the years they'd had together. It was Portia who had loved Chloe's father, too—just as it was Portia who had always rolled her eyes with her usual wisdom and good humor when Lao was around.

"My son was raised to take himself very, very seriously," she'd always said. "And heaven forfend those of us around him don't follow suit—the very fabric of the universe might be torn asunder."

Back then, it had not occurred to Chloe that it was *possible* to tease a man like Lao.

What she had understood, even as a small girl, was that it certainly wasn't *advisable*. And that the sort of teasing a man like Lao might accept from the woman who had given birth to him was likely not something that he would tolerate from anyone else.

But she tried that, too.

"You really must *try* to take yourself less seriously," she ventured one night. She even did her best impression of his mother. "Or you might actually turn into one of your bronzed statues, and then what will the grand Monteleone legacy do?"

As they had been walking along the castle's gallery, festooned with statuary in all directions, it had seemed like a reasonable thing to say. A bit funny, even. Especially as Lao was clearly in in a particularly glowering sort of mood and could do with some cheering up.

But she really wished she'd thought better of it when he looked at her in frozen amazement.

"I beg your pardon?" he asked, his voice soft in that way that meant he was on the verge of going fully incandescent.

And, because Chloe was at heart a coward when it came to this man, she cleared her throat. She felt herself wilt inside, and likely matched it outside, too.

"What I meant to say," she managed, "is that I'm not sure I fully understand your point? If you could repeat it?"

"I said what I always say." His dark gaze had been too brooding, too gray. "That when we began the real part of our marriage, I assumed that things would progress quickly."

"Bodies do as they like, regardless of our assumptions," she replied breezily.

"That is all well and good, but it is come September and you are not pregnant. Are you?"

"I am not," she agreed, when what she thought was *September*.

How had she missed the fact that she'd passed her three-month cutoff?

"We will fly to London in two days," he informed her coolly. "There is a doctor I wish you to see."

And that was it, then.

Chloe had to stop pretending.

He didn't love her, and there was no quiet way off this mountain—even if she'd wanted to go. There was no nipping out for a paper and failing to return. She didn't feel trapped, because how could she feel trapped when the man she loved was here?

But a trip to London meant her time was up. She already knew what his doctor would tell him, patient privacy be damned.

She'd had her experiment. She'd experienced more than she could possibly have imagined, going in. Surely she would find a way to be happy about that.

And in the meantime, it was time to leave him.

While she could still make herself go.

And before he learned what secret she had been keeping from him.

Chloe supposed that she'd known that the summer was ending, like it or not. There had been so many hints that she'd ignored. The breeze was no longer quite so soft. Some of the nights were downright chilly.

"London," she said faintly, focusing too intently on some or other bronze. "How lovely."

And she spent the time she had left saying her goodbyes.

To this marvel of the castle, stone and steel. To the tangled mystery of Sicily, these slopes and fields, groves and vineyards. The golden sunrises, like candy floss stretched across the horizon.

And in every spare moment, she said goodbye to Lao as well.

In the bed they had shared these last months. Sunk deep in that copper tub with its view of eternity. In the night, out near Portia's roses. She even took him by the hand and led him down that path he'd showed her on her first night here, down to that half-ruined watchtower, so she could show him all the things she had learned.

All the ways she had finally become his.

She didn't get much sleep, but that was a good thing. It allowed her to tell herself all manner of stories about why she was feeling so fragile when they finally boarded his plane. Or why, looking down at the castle and the whole of the island of Sicily from the air, she felt as if she was being torn in two.

You need a nap, she told herself, over and over again. *That's all.*

"You seem unusually subdued," Lao said as they soared high above the sparkling Mediterranean and headed north.

"I was thinking of the flight down months ago," she said, which was not a lie. She forced a smile, which was. "And how everything turned out so differently than I expected."

When he didn't respond, she glanced over at him, to see him studying her far too intently from across the table where they had taken their seats.

"Do you have a complaint that you would like to register?" he asked, his voice that mixture of mild disapproval and cool affront that made her sit up straighter even as it made the center of her need for him throb.

But today, maybe because she knew this was the end, it occurred to her that this was how this man who was raised to view feelings as a betrayal expressed his.

That felt like a revelation. She was almost tempted—

But no. He didn't love her. That was the beginning and the end of it.

"How could I have a complaint?" she asked lightly. "I am a Monteleone wife. Surely hordes fight daily for the honor. I am merely readying myself to defend my title on the streets of London."

Those steel gray eyes searched her face. And she felt as if he'd reached over and scooped out the contents of her chest, leaving her empty.

But no, said a voice inside her that sounded a

little too much like Portia's. *He has no need to do that. You are doing it for the both of you.*

"Very droll," Lao murmured in reply. "But it is no joke, Chloe. My only task in this life is to support my family's legacy, not diminish it."

"I know," she said, the words coming out on a rush of breath. And this time, the way she curved her lips was no lie. "I think you're lucky, really, to have been born with a purpose. Some of us wander about our whole lives and never find any. You had yours handed to you at birth. I understand that comes with its own set of challenges. But still, I think you really are lucky in the end."

"My father would be offended at such a notion," Lao said quietly, but there was something about the way he said it. Some kind of new, dangerous heat that lurked there, just beneath the surface. "He would say there is no such thing as luck. There is only strategy, power, and good breeding."

"He sounds like a fascinating man." Chloe waved a hand when Lao frowned at her. "What? I've always been fascinated by him. After all, he was the other ghost who hung over my childhood. And he was the one who mattered. I'm not sure my mother really counts, because, as far as I'm aware, she is still quite alive."

"Your mother lives on a lavish Bel-Air estate in Los Angeles," Lao told her matter-of-factly.

"These days she prefers a party circuit of well-placed lovers, who shower her with gifts because they think the settlement that pays her bills means she has some kind of power. All in all, I think she's quite as happy as she can be."

Chloe blinked. She let out a laugh, though it was involuntary. "That's…more information than I've had about Bianca in years."

"I started keeping track of her when my mother started dating your father. It seemed prudent, given her love of scenes and spectacles. And I continue to track her because she is, after all, the only living relative of my wife."

Lao raised a shoulder then lowered it as if in total unconcern, then returned his attention to his tablet and the work that waited for him at all times.

But Chloe…didn't quite believe he was as unconcerned as he pretended.

The trouble was, she knew him. She had known him for a long time. And the cold man who wished to compartmentalize everything and lock her away, his own Monteleone wife locked up in a tower awaiting his pleasure, was not the same man who had been surprisingly kind to a motherless girl.

She knew his mother. She had listened with avid attention over the years as Portia had told this or that anecdote about the boy Lao had been and the man he had become.

She knew the not quite stepbrother who had stepped in to take care of her when she'd been so lost in her own grief that she still didn't know what might have become of her otherwise or where she would be now.

And even now, with all his cool demands and orders, she still knew him. Looking back, she did not think she could possibly have surrendered to him so totally if she hadn't understood, down deep into her bones, that for all his thundering and all that steel, this man could never hurt her.

Hadn't she experienced that firsthand that night in the tower? When he had relieved her of her innocence and introduced her to a new version of herself she never would have found otherwise?

She was so different now, on this side of the most remarkable summer she'd ever had.

Chloe thought about her funny, brash, remarkable father and how open he'd been about his own mistakes. He had never savaged Bianca, but he'd made it quite clear that in his first marriage, he had allowed himself to be swayed by external factors. A mistake he had not made twice.

She thought about Portia, who had clearly suffered in her role as Monteleone wife and had made it clear, every single day she was with Chloe's father, that she had never been so happy before.

She thought of Lao himself, the way she always

did. The way she'd been thinking of Lao since she was a kid. And maybe she was the one at fault here, looking for signs of love from him that he could not give. Not because he didn't feel things, but because he didn't know how to show them.

Then again, she told herself sternly, *maybe he just doesn't love you.*

She felt that churn about inside her, making her feel sick to her stomach. Because the truth was, she didn't want that to be true. She didn't *want* to leave him.

All she needed was the tiniest little sign and she would stay forever, living off the crumbs of Lao's affections, such as they were. It was clear to her now that he had intended she do exactly that from the start. He had sex with her to keep her quiet, to keep her content.

And the passion between them was real, she had no doubt on that score. It was overwhelming and it was glorious and she did not think that she would ever quite recover—

But that didn't make it love.

Lao had told her enough about his childhood for her to know that none of his reasons for the things he said he wanted were good ones.

He wanted an heir because his family legacy required an heir, not because he had looked at Chloe one day and wondered what it would be like if the two of them created another little being made of bits and pieces of the both of them.

The only thing he cared about was his legacy.

He had told her so himself, hadn't he? A thousand times.

She could sit here and argue herself into thinking that he said such things—even thought such things—because he didn't know any better. Naturally, she was tempted to believe that all he really needed was someone to love him.

And she could already feel herself wilting inside.

After all, it had only been a short summer. It would take years to love a man like him enough to wash away his past. Was she running away too soon? He would be upset about the birth control shot, sure, but he would get over that. She was sure he would.

But she couldn't quite convince herself.

And she might have been the dozy cow Mirabelle liked to call her, but she knew one thing beyond a shadow of a doubt. Chloe still might not know what she wanted to do with her life. She might have meant it when she told him that he was lucky that he had a purpose.

Chloe might not know a whole lot of things, but she knew that she mattered. And more, that she was supposed to matter to the people in her life.

She would love Lao forever, if he would let her, and she didn't even require that he do it the way she might.

What she did need was to know that he could love her. That he *wanted* to love her. She did need that little bit of encouragement.

She also knew that Lao was not going to give it to her.

And so, in the end, it was easier than it should have been, because he expected her to remain docile. *Dozy.* She had given him no indication she would ever be anything but.

He took a call in one of his gleaming, luxurious limousines as they pulled up outside the doctor's office. He waved her inside,

Chloe marched into the lobby and was halfway to the appropriate lift before it occurred to her that this was the chance she had been waiting for. And even then, she hesitated. She looked back outside, toward the car…

But another thing her father had told her, especially after Portia died, was that life was for living, like it or not. And no one ever claimed that living was fair.

So instead of going up the lift to meet a doctor who was sure to tell her husband exactly why she wasn't pregnant, she walked through the lobby until she found a different door. Then she slipped out onto a different street and walked away.

She chucked her mobile, then presented herself at the nearest bank, where she withdrew a significant amount of money in hundred-pound notes. She bunged it all in a bag from the boutique next door, then bought herself a ticket on the first train heading north.

Mirabelle or one of her other friends would have been only too happy to let Chloe stay with her, but Lao was sure to look at her friends. And if she was honest, she didn't want to explain her summer to them. She didn't even know how she would begin.

Funny story, I've actually been married for five years? Yes, you know him. I mean, you know of *him...*

She didn't want to reduce what had happened between her and Lao to a silly story she could tell over drinks. The very idea made her feel a bit sick.

Within an hour, she was chugging out of King's Cross, with the ticket that would get her all the way to Aberdeen.

Eventually.

It was raining, and that felt right, so she sat by the window and stared out at the row houses she passed in London neighborhoods she'd never visited. Then, as the train sped north, she saw whole towns and small cities filled with *lives*. Filled with people with purpose, and people without any, all of them hunkered down and *living* in the same cold rain.

She told herself it was a comfort.

She was almost convinced it really was.

Chloe got off the train in the first place that she looked at and thought, *I wonder what it's like to live here* instead of *who can possibly live like that.* It seemed like the right distinction to make. It was already dark, and the September night was much wetter and colder in Scotland than it had been Sicily. But she found her way to a hotel and stayed there that first night, where she curled herself up in the narrow bed and sobbed herself to sleep.

It took her very little time to find a little bedsit in the city center—as it was amazing what cash in hand could do—and then she found a job waiting tables in a café, because it was that or spend her days becoming one of those ghosts she'd made it clear she wanted nothing to do with.

Every hour without Lao, she could feel herself becoming more and more see-through, as if she was disappearing by the day.

Yet the more she did a thankless job she didn't really fancy, the more she daydreamed about what she might prefer instead. Maybe infinite choice was a recipe for disaster. Maybe she would have been better off if her father had been strict with her. If he'd laid down the law about all the things she had to do and achieved to please him.

Maybe she could have had something to rebel against. Maybe that would have changed things.

But her father had loved her to distraction and had denied her nothing, and she knew that now the same as she'd known it then. With that same certainty and love. Just as she knew that if he hadn't, she would never have managed to do the necessary thing and walk away from a man who she might tell herself loved her madly—but he didn't want to.

And he would never say so anyway.

Chloe had to think that the bare minimum requirement she should accept from a man she was married to—especially one she had such intense chemistry with, which was really just a shortcut— was that he make her feel that kind of love. Not a father's love, but that kind of expensive, fundamental love, or what else was there to build life on?

Every day at the café, where she was in no way a great waitress, she gave herself rousing, private speeches about what she would and would not accept. She believed every word.

Still, she wavered.

The nights were the hardest. And she found that she'd become a bit of a night owl, because she did just about anything she could to stay awake. It was that or fall asleep and lose herself in those dreams. Dream after dream of the things she and Lao had gotten up to together. The taste of him in her mouth when she woke. The ache in her body because she wanted him so badly.

Sometimes she woke with tears pouring down her cheeks, sobbing, on fire, and so lonely she thought it might break her in half.

She *wavered*, and she was half ghost already, and it would be so easy to ring Lao the way she'd rung him a hundred times before. All she'd need to do was whisper his name and he would come to her.

He would save her from having to live with the choices she'd made. He would take her over and she would let him and she could convince herself all over again that he really was her purpose—

When he didn't want to love her, he just wanted babies. And obedience.

Chloe would never know what she might have done if she hadn't started feeling ill.

At first she just felt heavy. Then she began to feel nauseated at the strangest times. The smell of the food in the café where she worked could suddenly set her off. A meal she been living on—beans on toast, say—suddenly tasted revolting in her mouth. And maybe she knew what that might mean. Maybe she didn't want to know.

Maybe she was her own wishy-washy self to the bitter end.

But when she found herself waking up in the mornings and having to race to the toilet to heave up her empty stomach, she knew.

She didn't need confirmation. She rinsed her mouth, then walked the two steps out into the middle of her little bedsit, her head spinning.

Yet even as it spun, her hands crept over her belly, and she felt herself…exhale.

A sense of calm seemed to envelop her where she stood, in a little city in Scotland, a stranger to everyone she encountered.

And she didn't feel the slightest bit of *wavering* at all.

She was going to have a baby. And she was Chloe Stapleton, Charlie Stapleton's much loved only child. Even if Lao could claim half of the fortune she'd had him manage, the other half was hers. And it was more than enough.

She thought about Bianca and whatever high life her mother thought she was living. She thought about Portia, who had walked through a fire and then had lived out the rest of her days in joy.

All this time, she hadn't understood. She hadn't *known*.

But now she did.

She was going to be a mother. And she knew

that some women, having left their husbands and taken themselves off into strange and unlikely circumstances, would be scared. She would have been scared six months ago.

Yet today she was anything but.

Chloe had never felt a greater sense of purpose in her life.

This baby deserved all the things that Chloe had always wanted, and had only partly gotten. This baby deserved the world.

And Chloe intended to give it to her or him.

Whether Lao loved her or not.

CHAPTER NINE

LAO WOULD HAVE SAID, with the greatest confidence, that Chloe could not possibly evade him for a day. Much less an entire month.

And certainly not two.

Then again, he would also have said, with the same amount of confidence, that she would not *wish* to do anything of the kind.

Yet it was November when he finally got the call that he had been waiting for.

She had been sighted at last. After pulling off her exit from his life with an ease that made him wonder if he'd ever known her at all, she had reappeared in the same manner, as if in a puff of smoke. He waited, certain she would contact him the way she always had—

But she did not.

Moreover, she did not come back to Sicily, alive with apologies and explanations. She did not make any attempt to contact him at all. If he had not set his men in all the places he could think she might show, he might never have known, as he did not spend a great deal of time roaming about the neighborhood of that grand old estate outside of Winchester where Chloe had grown up.

Lao was tempted to conclude that his people were incorrect and it was not Chloe at all—but they were certain. And they had proof. Photographic evidence of a woman who was very clearly his missing wife, out for a walk in a misty British morning.

As if she had not abandoned him on a London street without so much as a backward glance. He knew. He had seen the CCTV footage.

And so Lao flew north from Sicily, consumed with that same rage they had eaten him alive since he had walked into that doctor's office and discovered that she had run off.

That rage that had been hot and bright and all-encompassing at first, but now it was…colder.

And it grew more frigid with every kilometer, he rather thought, as he sat in the back of the car that carried him through the frozen countryside of this bitter island she called home. This island she unaccountably preferred to his.

He could admit, if only in the privacy of his own head, that he had not spent these months without her gracefully.

Lao had spent three months with her, trying his best to keep her at a distance despite the demands of his own hunger. Then the next three without her, as much distance as it was possible to have, and he...had hated it.

The castle he had fashioned so that he might never live in misery, the way so many generations of his family had done in the manor house, had betrayed him. He found himself listening for her light, quick steps in the halls. He woke, certain he heard her laughter, only to find himself alone. His body had become conditioned to her touch, and he was appalled to discover that he missed it almost more than he could bear.

That he missed *her*.

Her absence was more of a distraction than her presence had ever been, and Lao, who had dedicated his life to being precisely the same man every Monteleone heir had always and ever been, was terribly afraid that he was forever altered.

At first, after ascertaining that she had not been abducted, he had not looked for her.

He had been certain that whatever might have spurred her to run from him, she would call him within the week, filled with shame and almost too flustered to talk. He imagined all the ways he would accept her back, how magnanimous he would be, and exactly what recompense he would demand from her sweet body.

But she did not call.

At the end of September, he'd sent his men off to find her, certain he would discover that she was languishing in some friend's villa somewhere warm and undemanding. Or, if not, perhaps haunting an art museum or gallery somewhere, talking of perspective and chiaroscuro with great passion to the unwary.

But she was in none of the places he thought she might be.

She was nowhere at all, though his men tracked her to a northbound train headed out of London. Eventually, they found that she'd exited that train in Scotland. Lao had spent the better part of October fielding reports from his men as they traced her through the Scottish hinterland, never finding her—but finding where she'd been. She had stayed the night in a questionable hotel. She had rented a sad bedsit above a chip shop. She had become a waitress in what the British called a kind of café, though it bore no resemblance to any kind of café Lao might frequent in Italy.

If he ever frequented cafés, that was.

Every day, Lao was forced to face the unpalatable fact that he clearly did not know Chloe at all. Because the Chloe he did know would never have managed to conceal herself. She would not have thought to use only cash, so as not to be easily traced. She would certainly never have lowered herself to bedsits and cafés that served only weak coffee and fried food.

She would not have known that she could bank on no one recognizing her, because no one had been looking for Chloe Stapleton, late of the society pages, in a grubby little town of stone and rain so far from any part of her actual life.

It was impossible not to take it as an insult.

That she should go from Castello Monteleone to living a life a bare shred above the poverty level—willingly and deliberately—was an affront. Though Lao could not pretend that he did not know that what outraged him the most was that he hadn't found her while she'd done these things.

Or that she was clearly no longer bothering to hide, which was the only reason he'd found her now.

He gritted his teeth and reminded himself that his temper had cooled. That it needed to stay cool.

But that was difficult to manage as he started to recognize the landmarks outside his windows.

Lao couldn't say he was pleased with this unwanted trip down memory lane he was forced to take as his driver navigated the increasingly familiar route to the old stately home where his mother had gone to live—with unseemly haste, in his opinion—after Portia and Charlie had gotten together.

This despite Lao's misgivings.

"You hardly know this man," Lao had argued when she had found him on the grounds of the castle, talking plans with his architect. She had chosen her moment deliberately, he knew. Because as little predisposed as Lao ever was to making a scene, his appetite for such things when there were witnesses was zero. "If you must date, Mother, surely you can do so without setting up domestic arrangements at the drop of a hat."

"Lao," Portia had replied, smiling in that way she had had…as if she was made up of too many secrets he could never possibly know. "I was not asking for your permission or even your blessing, though I would like it if you care to offer it. I was telling you what is happening, blessing or not."

She would not hear any arguments. There had been nothing for it. His mother had been remarried again before that year was out instead of living out her days as his *nonna* had done, wearing black only and asserting her will by whatever means she could. That was all unfortunate enough.

Worse, Lao had found he had no option but to come to this house in the British countryside far more than he liked.

Because his mother had refused to return to Sicily. Ever.

And he could admit that he had blamed Charlie Stapleton for that. Though now, as his car turned in the long drive that led up to the great old house, he wasn't sure why. It wasn't as if he didn't have a good idea why his mother had left Sicily. Why she had been unhappy as a Monteleone wife.

Or why she had tried to burn the manor house down.

And as the car drew up before the house, he found himself thinking that he could see his way toward a spot of pyromania all too easily.

The last time he'd seen this old heap, it had been in pictures sent by his staff after they'd closed it up five years ago. Chloe had been down in London, flitting about from one flat share to another with interchangeably pointless school friends of hers. There had been no need to keep the house open, so he hadn't.

It was instantly clear to him from the lights cutting through the November gloom alone that the house had been reopened without his permission or knowledge. For at least as long as it took to get a house this size up and running. There was smoke curling from the chimney. He could even see through the windows, meaning the shutters had been opened wide and inside, the furniture had been uncovered.

It looked a lot like Chloe—*his wife*—had moved back in.

When Lao knew this to be impossible, for *he* most certainly did not intend to live in England in this lifetime or the next.

He didn't wait for his man to open the door. He was out, sucking in deep breaths of the frigid November air as he stalked up to the front door and tried to open it.

Unlike his castle, which was of course protected by gates much lower on the mountain, the door to the old house was locked.

And so it was that he, Lao Monteleone, was forced to stand about in the cold, ringing the bell as if he was no better than a traveling salesman. Hawking his wares from house to house and hoping not to be run off by dogs.

He expected Chloe to open the door.

Or to shout at him through it while refusing to open it, more like, as that seemed to be the incomprehensible path this was taking.

But instead, the same ancient butler Lao recalled from his many visits here over the years opened the door and managed to look at him with a particular English hauteur that made it perfectly clear that the butler, at least, did not approve of him.

The insult was so great that it was obviously intentional, and Lao took a moment to cast about for the correct thing to say. Something that did not involve the cold fury he could feel charging through his veins—

But the butler stepped back. Wisely.

"Mr. Monteleone," he said, by way of a frosty greeting. "Miss Chloe has been expecting you."

Lao then prowled through the old house in the butler's wake, not sure how he was meant to handle this increasingly bizarre situation. It had been a long while since he'd found himself outmaneuvered, if ever. And if he'd had to guess who it might be who would manage to leave him feeling as if he didn't know what was going on, he would not have chosen Chloe.

Not his lost Chloe, who had only ever seemed to find herself with him.

Perhaps, came his mother's serene voice inside him, *you are not quite as lofty as you like to think you are, my son.*

He chose to shove that aside.

Lao had spent entirely too much time in this house, close and crowded as it was—like all houses of its ilk. He would even say that all the time he'd spent here had helped him as he was designing the *castello*, because he had wanted the opposite of this particularly British experience with its small rooms and closed doors.

The butler seemed to slow down on purpose with every step, and Lao refused to give the man the satisfaction of indicating his own impatience. So he slowed too, though the last thing he needed was quite so close a tour of a place he had never cared for overmuch.

And he thought his jaw might shatter from the effort of clenching it as hard as he was by the time he was finally waved into a room he recognized only too well.

It was the atrium that his mother had made into a greenhouse here, so she might keep a garden all year long. And Lao had grieved the loss of Portia in too many ways to count. He might not have agreed with his mother's every choice, though he had understood them, on some level. Because for a long while, they had been the only allies each of them had. They had not needed to discuss in any detail what they'd lived through, because they had survived it together—if in different ways.

And when he had not been pondering what it meant for his family's legacy—which had then been his responsibility—that his mother had gone off and remarried in such haste, he had been able to admit that he'd enjoyed seeing her happy.

Maybe some part of him had even thought that if she could be happy, maybe there was hope for him, too.

Though Lao had long since dismissed that sort of thought as weak and unworthy of him. Men in his position did not concern themselves with *happiness*. There were far too many other important things to do.

Still, it felt like stepping into a little too much old grief tonight. Because all of his mother's plants were gone. Of course they were. But he had found her here a thousand times, flitting from worktable to window box, deadheading flowers, cutting back this growth or that, and sinking her hands into the rich earth in her collection of pots.

It took him a moment to realize that she and her plants were not here. That the figure standing at the windows, her back to him, was not Portia. Those were memories.

This room, empty and cold, was real.

"It feels wrong that there are no plants here, doesn't it?" Chloe asked, without turning to face him, and that only made it colder. "If I thought I could grow my own roses here in her honor, I would."

Lao took in the sight of his wife…hungrily. He took in every detail. Her dark hair tumbled down her back in wild abandon instead of the more structured styles she'd worn in Sicily. He hated that he…didn't hate it. And though it was not warm, her feet were bare. And she otherwise wore a body skimming dress that made him entirely too aware the curve of her bottom.

Remaining where he was, and standing still, began to feel like something of a heroic act when all he wanted was to get his hands on her.

"What is this?" He kept his voice low in the hope that might keep the driving pulse of his temper at bay.

It was unsuccessful.

"Symmetry," Chloe said quietly, still looking out into the afternoon mist. "Does this not feel familiar to you, Lao? Only this time, I am the one standing in a window and you are the one in the doorway with no idea what's happening. It isn't pleasant, is it?"

And for the first time in as long as he could remember, Lao laughed.

Then had the distinct pleasure of watching his wife's spine straighten, as if the sound was an assault.

An assault with goose bumps, he could see. Which meant she was not as coldly set against him as she wanted him to believe.

"You are my wife, Chloe," he reminded her, and there was no concealing his temper any longer.

He was not sure he'd tried. "I will tell you exactly what is going to happen. You will return to Sicily. You will resume your place at my side. And if you are very lucky, I might allow you to leave my mountain in another fifty years or so."

She turned around then, and he was struck at once by the way her dark eyes blazed. By that strange new expression she wore on her face. He hardly recognized it. Or her.

And he didn't like how that made his chest go tight.

"No," she said.

Very distinctly.

And for a moment, that was the only thing that he could focus on. That single syllable that hung there between them as if it alone might bloom here, in this greenhouse where so many other flowers had flowered before.

"I beg your pardon?" He spoke through his teeth.

"No," she said again, sounding even more defiant than before. Her chin rose. "And even though that is a complete sentence, Lao, I'll explain it to you. If you want me to come back to you, then you must say so. I will not be responding to orders or commands. If you have something you want from me, you can ask for it. You might or might not get it. But I can tell you right now that you absolutely will not get anything from me by acting as if you're my boss instead of my husband."

"I fail to see the difference."

Even as he spoke, his gaze was moving over her with that same consuming need, that same hunger—made worse by these months without her. He was drinking her in, making sure that she was precisely as he'd last seen her. That she was still his, whether she knew it or not.

But she was wearing that tight, stretchy dress.

And she was not the same.

That pulse inside him grew louder. It became a kind of drum.

Lao was crossing the room, bearing down on her before he knew he meant to move, and he could not imagine what look he must have had on his face. But he did not mind it when her eyes went wide.

"I hope you don't think you can intimidate me," she began, in a higher-pitched voice that suggested he could.

And there was a part of him that did not want to intimidate her at all—but that was lost in the wild drumming that had taken him over.

"I would suggest that you choose silence," he managed to say, his voice barely more than a whisper as he reached her.

He was not looking at her face. He was looking

at her breasts, heavier now and rounded. He was letting his gaze skim down the rest of that body he knew better than his own, immediately noting the slight protrusion of her belly. The thickening of her hips.

Lao kept going, backing her up until she was pressed against the glass. Even then he didn't stop. He kept on until he could plant one hand beside her head and then he leaned closer, testing the evidence that his eyes had given him with his hands.

He took one breast in his palm, and ignored the startled noise she made as he weighed it against his memory and found it heavier. Then he smoothed his way down the length of his torso until he could find the new little belly she was sporting.

He kept his hand there as he felt her breath pick up. As he felt the heat of her bloom.

As he raked his gaze back up to stare her full in the face.

"Tell me I am mistaken," he growled out at her, not sounding at all like himself.

And, for once, not caring.

"I don't know what you are, Lao. I never have. What I do know is that you should not go around manhandling people—"

"You are pregnant," he bit out as if he could not believe the syllables that were coming out of his own mouth, because he could not. Because the betrayal was so deep, the cut of it so intense, that he was surprised he could still stand. "You are *pregnant*, Chloe. You ran from me. You hid from me. What game can you possibly think you are playing?"

He assumed she would crumple at that. That she would tremble.

But to his surprise, she straightened from the glass behind her, and pushed his hand away. He thought she might try to run again, but instead she stood tall, tilted her chin back, and held his gaze.

Without, it seemed, a single shred of fear.

When he rather thought she should have been significantly more worried than she appeared.

"I am pregnant, yes," she agreed, sounding significantly—and offensively—more calm than he had. "And do you know what that means?"

"What it means," he growled at her, his body alight with her betrayal as if she'd struck him with lightning, "is that you have made a terrible mistake indeed."

He saw the first hints of uncertainty then, a flash of it in her dark eyes, but it was gone in an instant. And her chin rose higher.

"I'm going to be a mother," she told him, in that careful, distinct way he discovered he disliked intensely. "And I don't care about your family legacy,

Lao. I care about this child and the kind of life it will have. I'm not going to be like my mother. I'm not going to abandon this baby when things get difficult, or boring, or whatever her complaints were. That will never happen. And I'm also not going to turn this child into the kind of robot that your father made you. I'm not going to do it and I'm not going to let you do it, either."

"Robot? You think I'm a *robot*?" He laughed again, a little more wildly this time. "You can say this despite all the many ways I have showed you that I am made entirely of flesh and blood?"

He could remember them all. Every touch.

He could see that she did, too.

But she said, "I've had a lot of time to think," instead of acknowledging what was between them.

And he had seen many versions of Chloe over the years. That cross little girl. That grief-stricken teenager. That sweet wife he'd had for so short a time, filled with wonder and need.

It settled in him like some kind of reproach that this was the first time he'd looked at her and seen the grown woman she had somehow become without him realizing it. No longer simply pretty, but objectively beautiful—with strength in her gaze and conviction in the set of her shoulders.

He felt it inside him like some kind of shudder.

Chloe was studying him with a kind of wisdom that Lao did not like at all.

"You don't want to know, do you?" she asked softly.

"Clearly," he belted out, "you have had entirely too much time to think. I cannot recommend it."

And he was not thinking at all when he reached out, his hand around the back of her neck, jerked her close, and then slammed his mouth to hers.

Lao was not thinking. He was *feeling*—and he knew better than that.

But this was Chloe.

This was Chloe, and so the kiss was not simply a kiss.

It was an explosion.

This was Chloe, *his Chloe*, and so the instant, impossible conflagration swept them both away. Their mouths clashed, tangled. Her hands were beneath his shirt, her fingers grazing his chest, her fingernails leaving little pinpricks of pain that only made it better.

This was Chloe, and her body had changed, so he had to learn her all over again. He bent to put his mouth to these new breasts of hers, full and ripe. He kissed his way down to her slightly rounded belly, so he might worship her.

And this was Chloe, so she fought him—but not to get away.

To get closer. Her hands fumbled with his belt. Her breath was coming fast and loud. And she sank down before him on the hard floor, pulled length of him from his trousers, and then took him deep into her mouth.

The way he had taught her.

It had been too long. It was too good. His hips moved of his own accord, the pleasure so intense, so hot and wet and *good*—

But Lao wanted more. He wanted everything.

He pulled her off of him and then up to her feet, but that wasn't enough. So he lifted her up right there, in the center of this atrium that had once been alive with green things and blossoms. He yanked up that dress of hers up to pool around her waist, pulled her legs wide around his waist, and then impaled her where they stood.

Her body made the shape of a bow. Her head fell back.

And Lao felt the fist of her sex piston around him.

Then she came apart.

Again and again.

She came and she came, and only when she was soft and writhing did he begin to move her, up and then down again, and she kept coming. And with every stroke, the fire roared through her and through him, burning them both alive.

At last.

But it still it wasn't enough.

It still wasn't everything.

Even when she locked her ankles around his back, grinned down at him, and whispered, "Catch up."

Not even when he did, with a roar.

And then moved back toward the windows so he could brace himself there. Then set her on her feet.

He was still bracing himself as she caught her breath beside him, her whole body shaking.

But her gaze was sad when she looked at him.

"Does that not convince you?" he managed to say.

Something in him stuttered, then stopped, when she reached over and smoothed one hand over his jaw. With that same heaviness in her dark gaze.

"We've always been good at that, haven't we?" she asked softly. "But look around, Lao. This atrium used to be filled with joy and love and light. Your mother spent hours in here, encouraging all of her plants to grow. To bloom. She would cut flowers and arrange them all over the house. There was no part of her life that didn't share in this happiness."

"Chloe."

He said her name in desperation, as if it was

torn from the very heart of him—as if he had such a thing after all—but she didn't stop.

"Now it is empty. It is an old glass room that feels drafty. The floors are cold and hard. And nothing grows here any longer."

"Because the house was closed up." He didn't recognize that dark urgency in his own voice. Or the feeling in his chest, as if his ribs were against him. "If you wish there to be a garden here, I could easily see to it that there is always—"

"If I wanted a garden made out of money, I could buy one myself."

And it would have been one thing if she sounded angry. Or even bitter, but she didn't. Once again, she sounded nothing but sad.

For you, a voice inside him whispered.

"Tell me what you want," he urged her, his voice a growl. "Name it, and I will give it to you. I will get you ever flower in Europe."

"It's not the flowers that matter. It's how they were grown." She waited, as if she needed him to say something to that, but all he could do was stare back at her, his heart a mad riot within him. "Love. They were grown with *love*, Lao. So will this child be grown inside me."

"I don't understand." The words tasted like ash in his mouth, but he pushed on. "Did I not take care of you, for years? Was I not there for you when you had no one else? Is this how I am repaid?"

"I love you," she told him, the way she had once before.

And this time, she looked him full in the face. She didn't blink.

Lao did not know how he was meant to handle this. This…*outrage*. He kept telling himself it was nothing more than that.

And she wasn't done. "I think I have always loved you. I expect I always will. All I ask is that you care a little bit less about your legacy and a little bit more about the possibility that you might just love me back. Whether you know it or not."

He stared back at her, his chest heaving as if he suddenly found himself running a marathon. "And if I cannot?"

Though the words hurt.

She smiled again, though there was nothing but that same sadness in it. A sadness he could feel inside him, winding its way through him like too much smoke.

When he thought he'd extinguished that kind of fire a long time ago, and for good.

Her smile only grew sadder, as if she knew.

"Then I am afraid that you will have to go," she said, with a deep certainty that was almost more of an earthquake within him. Because he had never heard Chloe—his Chloe—speak like this before. With such offhanded authority. She hugged her own belly, where their child grew even now. And she meant every word she aimed at him, with devastating precision. He could tell. "Because I will not raise this child—our child—without *at least* as much love and joy, hope and delight, that your mother gave her plants. I won't even try."

CHAPTER TEN

THIS WAS THE hardest thing that Chloe had ever done. With every breath, she wanted to snatch her words back. She wanted to tell Lao that she didn't mean them. That however he might take her, however he might treat her, it was good enough.

Because it was better than not being with him at all.

And she might have done exactly that, before. She'd been wavering. She'd been weak, and she knew that.

If he had shown up at that little bedsit of hers in Scotland, who knows what might have happened? Well. She did know. He would have had her back in Sicily so fast her head would have spun. He would never have let her off that mountain again. She would have become yet another Monteleone ghost.

But instead, she'd found herself pregnant, and that had changed everything.

It had changed *her*.

"You talk freely of love for someone who, in the next breath, threatens to leave me, with my child, if I do not dance to your tune," Lao thundered at her. "What kind of love do you call this, exactly?"

"What does it matter?" She didn't know how she was keeping her voice so calm, when everything inside of her shook so hard. "Whether it's a good love or bad love, you don't want any part of it. So no need to concern yourself with it either way, I would think."

Her body was still reacting to what had happened between them here, and that didn't help. She was melting, still, and she could feel that same mad passion ramping up inside her all over again, the way it always did when she was near him.

But the one slip was all she would allow herself.

Because they were other things to think about now.

She brushed past him, and marched toward the door, feeling slightly ashamed that it was wide open. Any of the staff could have seen them in here—and given that they'd all helped raise her, the very idea made her face flame.

But she didn't let that stop her. She made her way to the warmer parts of the house, that she could keep at any temperature she liked, now, and she didn't know if that made her want to laugh or cry. Her father had always complained about how warm the place was, at least until Portia had become ill, when he'd stopped complaining about anything.

She reminded herself that today, here and now, the baby she carried was the only thing that mattered.

Not who she missed. Not what the people who worked here could have seen. Not Lao, not her. Just the baby who she intended to make sure lived the happy life she and Lao had only ever had pieces of.

If that.

She went into the room that Portia had claimed as her retreat in this house, aware that Lao was following her, his frustration plain in every step.

It was a cold, dark, November afternoon day outside and the fire was crackling merrily in the grate, making the spines of all the pretty books on the shelves lining the walls seem brighter. The old butler who had served her father so well had taken charge the moment Chloe had tracked him down, opening up the house, bringing back the rest of the old staff, and doing the place up as Chloe had always liked it best.

Meaning that a lovely cream tea was already waiting for her here, in the very room Portia had taught her to love them as a child.

But Chloe didn't go and sit on the happy little couch, she went to the bookshelves instead, running her fingers over the much-loved volumes that Portia had always stacked haphazardly on the shelves, claiming that a neat bookshelf was a sign of a disordered soul.

"You know this was your mother's favorite room, don't you?" she asked Lao softly.

"I have been in this room many times, Chloe. As you are well aware. And I do not see what my mother's preferences have to do with this."

Chloe turned, her lips curving into something that wasn't quite a smile. "Do you not? Really?"

She had never seen Lao quite like this. His eyes were a wild quicksilver and for the first time in as long as she'd known him, he seemed to…*simmer*. As far from that cold, stern, and forbidding presence as it was possible to get without outright exploding.

And the way he looked at her made her think that all that thunder that was normally in his gaze was in her now. Sunk deep into her bones.

She was not sure she would ever get it out again. Or even if she wanted to.

Chloe kept her hand pressed against her belly, as if that could soothe the child inside. *We will be all right*, she promised the baby silently. *You and I will make it work, whether we are made of thunder or not.*

"Tell me what I have done to you, please," Lao

grated out at her. "You disappear on the way to a doctor's appointment. You hide yourself in Scotland under an assumed name. You conceal the heir you know I have wanted for some time from me. Is this how you repay my kindness to you? A kindness you were once so grateful for that you offered to carry my child when there was no physical relationship between us?"

Chloe pressed her fingers into her belly a bit more firmly. "I will always be grateful for your kindness to me, Lao. This has nothing to do with that."

"This has everything to do with it." He had been standing in the door, but he came in further now, and in one step seemed to take it over. The little room, peaceful and happy as it has always been, seemed to disappear into him. As if he was a black hole that dragged everything it encountered deep inside of him.

She felt that same irresistible pull herself.

"I had no intention of getting pregnant," she told him, and maybe her voice was a little less calm, now. In the face of that intoxicating pull. And Lao getting that much closer, making it hard to concentrate. She cleared her throat and reminded herself that this wasn't about her. "I know that was your goal, but it was never mine."

"What, pray, did you think would happen?" Lao

shook his head, his eyes glittering. "I shudder to think what will become of you, Chloe. So lost, even now. And so unable to understand the very basics of human anatomy."

He might as well have slapped her. She felt as hot and furious, as wounded.

"I was on birth control, Lao," she snapped back at him. When she saw him take that in, his head jerking back as if she was the one who had landed a blow, she felt something in her light up. Like that was some kind of triumph. "Do you really think I'm that stupid?" But she let out a small laugh. "Don't answer that. I can see that you do. You truly believe that I'm such a fool that I would imagine I could have that much sex with you— with anyone—while taking absolutely no precautions, and imagine nothing would come of it?"

She expected him to fire back, and wasn't sure what to do when he only sighed, muttering something in Italian beneath his breath. "I do not think you are stupid. I assumed you wanted the same things that I did."

"You know that I didn't," she replied, her voice fierce. Because whatever that little pop of triumph was, it quickly turned into this. This bright fire inside her. "You knew all along how much I loved you, and what a dream come true it was to me that I could have you in that way. It never crossed your mind that you shouldn't use your power and your influence to get exactly what you wanted, and you know what the funniest part of this is, Lao? I don't mind that. Some part of me *likes* it. Because I know exactly who you are. I love you exactly as you are."

"Even as we stand here, discussing your lies," he said in that quietly furious voice of his that should not have affected her as much as it did. "You can understand, can you not, how pale the words sound in these circumstances?"

"I love you," she said again, and she didn't care if he could hear the fire in her. The fire she wanted very much to be temper, not need. "I love you, Lao, but not enough to set aside every weapon at my disposal. Not enough to give myself over to you like some virgin sacrifice and help you burn me to a crisp in some ritual fire."

"Monteleones have not required ritual sacrifices in some centuries, Chloe."

"But the result is the same," she threw at him. "Is that really what you want? Because sometimes, there's something else inside you, Lao. I've seen it." Or she liked to think she had. "Something more than the Monteleone legacy. There's more to you than that. I know there is."

His jaw worked. His eyes blazed.

When he spoke again, his tone was frozen solid. "You are mistaken."

"I'm sorry to hear that," she shot right back at him. "Because I will not allow you to flatten this child the way you were flattened."

More of that silver fire, aimed directly at her. "I would not call it *flattening*. I was raised very differently than you, Chloe. I was given responsibilities at a very young age and asked to live up to them. I was not coddled. No one cooed over me or applauded when I ran about, doing as I liked."

"Your mother did all of those things," she replied softly. "All your life. It's just that she was overruled."

It was like a new storm broke then, washing over Lao and making him…a whole electrical event. He scorched the sky, the room, *her.*

Chloe's pulse was skyrocketing through her veins.

His voice was so quiet it hurt. "You have no idea how I was raised."

"I do." She indicated the room around them. "Your mother used to tell me all about it, right here. Usually after you visited and she felt she had to make excuses for…" She waved her hand at him. "The way you are."

"The way I am?" He said the words in his typical affronted astonishment, but today it was worse.

Today it burned. "By this you mean… What, dare I ask?"

"Shuttered," she shot back at him immediately. "Locked up inside yourself. Grim and forbidding and off-putting, as if, when you were still a young man, you had already made yourself over into some hermit on a mountaintop—counting your piles of money while the world turned on without you." She let out a small laugh at the expression on his face. "Those aren't my words, Lao. They were Portia's."

He moved closer then, so close that his scent seemed to wrap itself around her, teasing her. Tempting her.

It would be so easy to simply melt against him. To wrap herself in his arms and forget what she was trying to do here. What she knew she *needed* to do. Because she was standing here in Portia's favorite retreat, the one her stepmother had made after leaving Sicily and the Monteleone legacy behind. So Chloe already knew how this would end, didn't she?

She couldn't pretend she didn't, no matter how much she longed for Lao even now.

"I think you're relying too heavily on the words of a woman who wanted, very desperately, to create a tidy narrative of her own past." Lao did not exactly spit those words out, but they were like bullets, one after the next, slamming into her as he towered above her. "I am not certain my mother was the woman you wish she was, Chloe. Then again, I'm not sure anyone could be."

"Are you really going to try to convince me that your mother was…" She shook her head, feeling as if the room was suddenly spinning a little too fast all around her. "I don't even want to know what sort of twisted attempt this is to—"

"Do you know why I tore down the manor house?" There was something different in him, she could see it. He seemed to blaze at her, then. A lightning strike that just kept coming. "Because she did not merely burn down the wing she shared with my father. She went on a rampage, ransacking the place, and it was easier to take it all down then to repair it. Does that strike you as the actions of a well-adjusted woman?"

"Maybe she was a desperate one," Chloe whispered.

"My father was already dead." He bent toward her, his face as cold as his eyes were hot. "I assumed my mother was having a breakdown, so when she left the island—claiming she was going abroad for some rest and recuperation—I supported it. Instead, she announced she was marrying your father. And quickly."

"Yes," Chloe said, though it took everything she

had to keep standing there, defying him, when it would be so much easier to simply... Melt the way everything in her wanted to do. "Because whatever else you might think about my father, or whatever you thought of him then, what's undeniable is that he made Portia feel safe. For the first time in her life, I think. That means something."

The strangest expression moved over his face then. Lao stepped away from her, which should have pleased her. It didn't.

Then, in one of the few hints she'd seen outside the bedroom that he was, indeed, a mortal man, he rubbed his hands over his face as if this conversation was finally getting to him.

Chloe couldn't decide if she was pleased about that or not.

"Do you really believe..." Lao shook his head, then wheeled around to scowl into the fireplace, though she doubted he was seeing the flames before him. "My mother was raised on a silver platter, wrapped in cotton wool, not too far from where we stand right now. She came from a very long line of proper English heiresses, all of them trotted out to marry this or that lord on command. Or, if he is of high enough status, not necessarily marry him at all. One of her direct ancestors was a particular favorite of one of your King Georges, or so her family like to claim." He turned back then, and she would have called the look in his eyes a kind of anguish, except he seemed so icily furious. "My point to you is that my mother was not some…random commoner who was swept up into a world she could not understand. She was bred for the role she took. From the time she was born, she and her sisters were raised to marry a very specific sort of man and become a very specific sort of wife. There was no expectation of a happy love match, an egalitarian relationship, God forbid, or anything other than maintaining the family profile and giving herself over to her husband's demands."

Chloe felt as if she was shaking apart from the inside out. "How unfortunate that instead of being an automaton, she was Portia."

"You are speaking of who she became," he told her in that same stormy way. "I'm speaking of who she was. Whether she liked her duty or did not, the vows she took meant she continued to do it. I'm not going to stand before you and pretend that my father was a kind, softhearted man. I do not believe that he ever pretended otherwise. It was my mother who changed. She could not accept that he would not change with her."

"Yet somehow, you're telling me this story to blame her, not him."

"Because she is the one who did not live up to her commitments," Lao threw at her. "She is the one who was forever bleeding her emotions everywhere, making nothing but a mess. And to what end? Nothing changed. Certainly not my father, who died as he lived, stern and uncompromising to the very end. And even then, my mother let her emotions lead her into appalling displays. Involving fire and wanton destruction. If she were anyone else but *my mother*, she would have been thrown in prison for arson. Rightly."

"Lao," Chloe managed to say, though she felt as if she was rattling apart. As if some sort of earthquake had started, right here in Winchester, and soon enough the fault would swallow her whole and leave nothing behind but rubble. Still, she tried to focus on the only thing that mattered here. "Lao, I think—"

"All she had to do was her duty," Lao thundered. "That's it. That's all that was ever asked of her, and it was too much. She had everything her heart could possibly desire. Money. Power. Influence. So many things that when she burned down half of them she still had more than plenty. I will never understand what made her think that she could change a thing. Or why she'd want to." She ran her hand over his face again. "What could she possibly have thought she could gain from going head-to-head with my father?"

"You," Chloe said, with a deep certainty she

could not possibly have explained. It had something to do with the baby inside her. With the new, proud jut of her own belly that made everything… clear. Maybe too clear. "She was hoping to gain *you*, Lao. She was losing her son, day after day, as you became more and more like him. Because you have, haven't you?"

She could see the way his chest moved as he stood there. She could see how wild and silver his gaze was.

"Portia was hoping to give you a choice," Chloe said, because she knew. She just knew. "To be like her or to be like him. And look what you've chosen. Look who you've become."

She had never seen Lao look so undone as he did then. So unlike himself.

And she wasn't sure she had ever loved him more—

But because of that, because of the baby she carried and had to protect above all things—even if that meant from him—she stayed where she was.

And no matter that it felt like she was hurting herself…

"Chloe…" he managed to say.

"Is fire what it takes?" she asked him then. "Is that what gets your attention."

"Chloe," he said again, with more force this time.

But she refused to listen. She stood with her

back straight and her gaze steady. "Tell me, Lao, what do I have to burn down to prove to you that I love you? Though I think we both know that's not the real question."

She thought he might argue further, but all he did was gaze back at her, as if she was haunting him.

Right here, in this happy room, in the middle of the afternoon.

"The real question," she made herself say, though it tore up her throat and seared her tongue, so desperately did she want to keep these words to herself, "is why you believe you can't love me back without the whole of Castello Monteleone falling straight off the mountain and into the sea?"

CHAPTER ELEVEN

IT WAS TOO MUCH.

There was a certain anguished *kindness* in Chloe's gaze—too close to pity, by his reckoning—and he couldn't take it. He couldn't allow it.

Instead, Lao found himself shouldering his way out of the room, then staggering through the cramped old house until he found himself outside in the cold.

He gulped in the damp air, as if that might save him.

As if that might make sense of these things raging inside him.

He thought of his father, never *quite* cruel, because true cruelty required a deeper level of attention than his father had ever given to anything that was not a part and parcel of the Monteleone estate.

His father, always talking of duty. Always making it clear that while Portia fell far short, it was still possible for Lao to prove himself.

If he worked hard. If he never strayed from the path laid out before him by his betters. If he got his unruly reactions to things he didn't like under control.

Lao had done all of those things and more, though he'd failed more than he'd succeeded, at first.

He'd gotten better at it after he'd been sent off to boarding school, where he'd received a crash course in locking up any stray emotions he might have attempted to have, lest they make him a target.

In time, he had forgotten he'd ever had any.

Just as he'd forgotten all the things his mother had told him that did not fit with his father's version of events.

"Why can't you stop?" he had asked her one night before his father had passed. After another dinner had gone south, in a hurry, because Portia had refused to sit there in the obedient silence his father required. "You know he won't divorce you. What is the purpose of defying him?"

"I do not have to stay here," his mother had replied. "This is not the only Monteleone property, as I think you know. I could live quite happily elsewhere."

"Then you should," he had returned, with all the arrogance of the younger man he'd been then, who had taken such pride in his inability to feel things the way Portia did.

He had told himself that the brightness he'd seen in his mother's gaze that night was her shame, not his.

And he remembered his father's deathbed, too. How his mother had tended to a man she could not possibly have esteemed in any way by that point. Without question, without a word.

A parody of the perfect wife she had never been, Lao had thought then.

Yet in the end, his father had laughed. His gaze had been something like feverish then, his body already so changed that though he had not yet died, he already looked far too much like a cadaver.

"The Monteleone legacy always wins," he had cackled. "Always."

Then he had closed his eyes, taken one, last rattling breath, and died.

And all this time, Lao had believed his father had been speaking to him. That he had been passing on one last piece of advice, one last directive.

It had never occurred to him that his father had been doing no such thing. He'd been taunting Portia.

This seemed so clear to him now. The old man had been drawing his last breath, he'd known it, and he'd used it to announce to his wife that he had made their son into the image of him.

More importantly, that there was nothing she could do about it.

And suddenly, that his mother had chosen to set fire to the part of that legacy she must have hated the most did not seem in the least bit surprising. Nor in any way the kind of breakdown he'd been so sure she was having.

How had it taken him all this time to understand that?

But he knew. It was Chloe.

He had spent so much time and effort convincing her that she needed him, when all along, it seemed it had been the other way around.

Lao had been paying no attention to where he was going, and it took him long moments to recognize that he was in the garden, hunkered down against the cold, though it was now, in late fall. The again, perhaps he'd meant to come here, he thought as he recognized his mother's rosebushes, cut back for winter.

To the untutored eye, they might even look dead.

But he knew better.

Because now, in a great rush of painful understanding, he knew why Portia had spent her days up in the castle ruins, tending to plants that died each winter and rose again each spring.

She had been fighting for him all along. She had been tending to him as best she could. Not, perhaps, doing her duty as a Monteleone.

But always—*always*—doing her duty as a mother.

Doing it so well that Lao had not even noticed what she did.

He reached down, brushing his hand over one of the withered-looking stalks—only to pull it back when his finger stung.

Somehow, it was as if the thorn that pierced his skin punched straight through him.

Lao saw a single red droplet of his own blood, there in the November gloom, and it was as if he was made new.

As if all the things that had seemed so out of control even an hour ago came suddenly back into focus.

Snapping off the bit of stem, he turned to make his way back up to this house that he had always told himself was too uncomfortable. Too English. He had always kept his visits short, to guard against too much of Charlie Stapleton rubbing off on him.

That was what he'd always thought. That was what he would have said—and probably had said—to his own mother.

Now he understood why she had always smiled so serenely, yet never engaged with him in the argument he'd clearly wanted.

Because she knew.

What he couldn't tolerate was love.

The love between Charlie and Portia. The love between Charlie and Chloe. The love his own mother lavished on the girl herself.

The love the Stapleton clan felt for their staff, who returned it in kind—and if he'd doubted that, it was proved well enough by the fact they had all come out of retirement to help Chloe now.

It wasn't that he couldn't tolerate all that love, he thought now. He hadn't even been capable of recognizing it for what it was.

No wonder Chloe had been so lost without it.

He found himself charging through the house once more, barely noticing the rooms that still looked sleepy from being closed up all these years. Barely noticing the canny-eyed old butler who nodded at him, or anything at all but the light that led him back the way he'd come.

The light that led him to Chloe.

She was where he'd left her in his mother's favorite room. While he'd been out facing reality in a stripped-down rosebush, she had taken herself over to the fire. She stood there, her arms wrapped around her middle, as if she was afraid that if she let go she might fly apart.

Or perhaps as if he had already broken her beyond repair.

She turned when he came in, and Lao had some sense of how it must seem to her that he should come charging back like this, the cold and the wet clinging to him as if he brought the coming night with him wherever he went.

He thought maybe he did. That he had done, and for years.

But this was Chloe, so what she did was take a look at him—a long, hard look, so that he expected her to order him away.

Instead she simply…opened up her arms, offering him nothing but that invitation and the sheen of a deeper longing in her gaze.

Because she knew exactly what love was.

And it was as if everything within him shattered to dust, that simply.

He came toward her, still gripping that strand of thorns in one fist. She made a soft noise when she saw it, and then her hands were on his. She was peeling open his palm, shaking her head as she peered down. "Lao. You're bleeding."

"But I can feel it," he said gruffly. "That must mean something."

She looked up, eyes wide and much too bright.

As he watched, she pulled the thorns from his hand and tossed them into the fire.

"You and I can agree that we should burn the things that hurt us," she told him softly. Solemnly. "But not the rest."

A single tear trailed down one cheek, and she leaned down to press her lips into the palm of his hand.

As if her kiss alone could soothe the cuts he'd made with the might of his own grip.

And the metaphor wasn't lost on him. The harder he held on to those thorns, the deeper they had pierced his flesh.

All it took was opening up his hand—and the one thing he didn't think he could survive losing was still right here, her lips against his palm, tears for him in her soft gaze.

"Chloe," he told her, though the words caught in his throat. "I think that you are the only thing I've ever loved."

"Not the only thing," she corrected him, with a smile that no longer seemed tinged with sadness. "Just the most simple thing."

He reached over with his unabused hand and smoothed it over her cheek, her hair. "There's nothing simple about you. And I love every part of you. Whether you are lost or found, as long as you are mine."

"Lao." She shook her head, and his stomach fell—until he saw the way her lips curved. "I always have been. Since I was all of seven, and you came to me, right here in this house, and made everything better."

"I doubt that. That is not the Monteleone way."

"But it's our way," she whispered, fiercely. "It has always been *our* way, if we let it."

And there, standing before the fire where the last of his mother's roses burned, yet would still bloom again come spring, Lao let go.

He opened himself up, and *let go.*

Lao let go of that wall he had been trying to build between himself and this woman…forever. He let go of the legacy his father had cared about above all else.

He let go of all the things that no longer seemed at all important and concentrated on this.

The woman who looked up at him with love and trust in her gaze, though he knew full well he had done nothing at all to deserve them.

The woman who carried his child in her body, and who had been prepared to fight even him to keep that child safe.

And he understood that this moment would be the one his whole life hinged upon. Everything that had come before, and everything that would come after—all of it depended on this.

On what he did now.

He could do his duty to a dead man who loved only his legacy, or he could do his duty to the child he already wanted to love with all his heart.

This was what his mother had known all along. He could not do both. No man could.

Not if he wanted to give his child the love that child deserved.

The love he knew Chloe had gotten from her father.

And of the two of them, it seemed obvious to him that she had come out better adjusted, with no Monteleone legacy like a noose around her neck.

So he gathered his beautiful wife in his arms. He held her there, before the fire.

"Chloe," he murmured. "*Dusci mia, sei tutto per me.* You are everything to me. I want you to marry me."

"I already have," she whispered.

"This time I want a spectacle," he declared, and this time when he felt his heart like a drum inside his chest, he called it joy. Hope. "I want to pry open my family's secrets and wash us all clean of the secrets and the lies. So that the only thing remaining is this. Us."

She looped her arms around his neck and tilted her head back while she looked at him, tears streaming down her cheeks.

But he knew that she was showing him love, complex and sweet, layered with too many feelings to count, right there before him.

He knew it was love. He could feel that, a brighter and better sting than any thorn could ever be.

"I promise you," she whispered. "I will be the best Monteleone wife there ever was."

"Mi amore," he replied, as he smoothed his hands over her belly, then raised them again to take her face in his. "Do you not see? You already are."

CHAPTER TWELVE

LAO WAS ABSOLUTELY true to his word.

He was a Monteleone, after all. But these days, he chose the legacies he wished to uphold.

He opened the whole of his mountain to the world. He tore down the ancient gates and invited them all in, with cameras aplenty, to witness his wedding to Chloe.

Because the only thing more powerful than the mystery of the age-old Monteleone legacy was love, and he intended to prove it.

The way Chloe proved to him, every day, that he was not the man he'd always thought he was.

She taught him how to laugh. She taught him how to *play*. She taught him that there was nothing to fear in the emotions he had tried to hold off his whole life—not while they were together.

Together they planted his mother's roses on his

father's grave, then left them to do as they liked. They planted trees in the ruins of the manor house.

"So that one day, another Monteleone will stand right here," Chloe said as they held each other in his office one day. "And see only the island and the sea."

"No ghosts," Lao agreed, like it was a vow.

Their son was born six months later, and once again, the whole world shifted. Once again, Lao found he had to reassess not only who he was, but how he had ever considered having an heir nothing more than a cold-blooded duty to check off his list.

"I cannot understand it," he told Chloe, mere days after the heir he had always wanted had been born into his hands. But he was no *heir*.

He was called Gaetano. He was a miracle.

Lao held his son against his chest, skin to skin, and was in love. He didn't care that this was his supposed successor. He didn't care that this was what his own father would have wanted.

The woman he loved more than he had ever loved anything or anyone on this earth had fought and struggled and brought forth their child into this world, and now, together, they had no job at all but to love him. To care for him.

To do their best to nurture him, for all his days.

To take part in this journey that would, God willing take little Gaetano with his chubby hands and sweet red face, from the bundle of heat and wailing he was today to the man he would become.

Lao intended to enjoy every moment.

"What can't you understand?" Chloe asked softly, curled up next to him on the soft couch. She had never looked more beautiful, still round from her pregnancy, her breasts big with milk. "How it's possible to love anything as much?"

They had made the room next to theirs, supposedly her bedroom, the nursery. Because there was no point pretending that they would ever sleep in separate beds. They sat there now, close together basking in this small, perfect life they had made between them.

"That, yes," Lao said quietly, playing with Gaetano's tiny fists. "But then to act as my father did."

Chloe traced a gentle circle on the tender, soft spot on the baby's head. "For all we know, he was gentle and loving compared to his own father."

"I promise you, Chloe," Lao grated out, because now he was a man made entirely of emotion. He was not afraid to let it grip him, hard. He was not afraid of what love wrought in him. Not as long as they went through these storms together. "I will never let that happen to us. Or to our son."

"I know you won't," she said, her lips on his.

But as much as he loved her belief in him, Lao made sure to work on it.

He worried less about power and influence. He created his own legacy, by beginning to give away the money that his ancestors had spent so long amassing to those who needed it.

And there were so many who needed it.

Not to mention, it turned out that Chloe had a particular talent for giving his money away. And, like him, wanted that to be the secret of the Monteleone family.

The only secret worth keeping.

And as the years passed, they spent their time together dispensing joy where they could, and spending as much time as possible together—and with the children they made.

The four he had rashly demanded, and two more, for fun.

"It is incredibly unfashionable to have so many children," he told Chloe when their sixth was a toddler, incredibly full of herself and entirely feral. Sebastiana was a terror in every respect—but that only made them love her more. "We are no doubt the laughingstock of Europe."

"Good," Chloe said. She covered her mouth to hide her laughter as red-cheeked, overly serious

Sebastiana spun too fast and toppled straight over on the grassy stretch of hill before the castle. Then howled with rage before picking herself up to do it again. When Chloe dropped her hand, her gaze was soft, but serious. "I don't want any of them to ever think they're alone in this world, Lao. Not like us."

Never like them.

That was the mantra that Lao lived by. That was the promise he made himself, day in and day out.

His children would not be alone. His children would have the both of them. His children would never question whether or not they were loved.

Chloe taught him that every day. Just as his own mother had tried, over and over again.

And every year, one slipping by after the next more quickly than seemed possible, Lao watched his mother's roses wilt in fall and then bloom again in spring.

Each year, brighter than the year before. Each year more beautiful and more fragrant.

And thorns were inevitable, but none too sharp or too painful—provided he knew the trick of letting go.

Of choosing love instead.

Over and over again, the way Chloe had taught him. The way he wanted to love his children, so well that they would never know another way.

So that the legacy that he and Chloe left, in the end, was a love so right, so good, it lasted as long as the roses bloomed on Castello Monteleone and their descendants were there to tend them.

Which was another way of saying forever.

* * * * *

Did the drama of
What Her Sicilian Husband Desires
have you longing for more?
Make sure to lose yourself in these other
captivating Caitlin Crews stories!

Reclaiming His Ruined Princess
Willed to Wed Him
The Christmas He Claimed the Secretary
The Accidental Accardi Heir
A Secret Heir to Secure His Throne

Available now!

COMING NEXT MONTH FROM

PRESENTS

#4113 MIDNIGHT SURRENDER TO THE SPANIARD
Heirs to the Romero Empire
by Carol Marinelli

For dedicated single mother Anna, attending her friend's Spanish wedding is a huge milestone. But as the clock strikes midnight, she surrenders to her chemistry with super-rich best man Sebastián. He can only offer one pleasure-filled night, but will Anna want more?

#4114 BACK TO CLAIM HIS ITALIAN HEIR
by Kate Hewitt

After surviving a plane crash, Nico returns to his wife, Emma, to discover three shocking revelations. First, he's presumed dead! Second, Emma is pregnant with Nico's child...and last, he must stop her convenient marriage to another man!

#4115 THE REASON FOR HIS WIFE'S RETURN
Billion-Dollar Fairy Tales
by Tara Pammi

Dutiful Mira's wedding to Greek billionaire Aristos was always a practical arrangement to have a child, nothing more. But when their explosive encounter felt powerfully real, Mira fled. Now she's back...and she's carrying Aristos's twins!

#4116 PENNILESS CINDERELLA FOR THE GREEK
by Chantelle Shaw

Years ago, Dimitris wasn't considered good enough for heiress Savannah. But when the penniless photographer seeks his help, he'll offer her a job in Greece. Their chemistry is still combustible, but can he risk rekindling anything other than their desire?

#4117 HER VOW TO BE HIS DESERT QUEEN
Three Ruthless Kings
by Jackie Ashenden

Khalil ibn Amir al-Nazari never forgot the marriage pact innocent Sidonie Sullivan scribbled on a napkin five years ago. Now, he'll enforce it to save his kingdom! But can he convince Sidonie that he wants her for herself too?

#4118 PREGNANT AT THE PALACE ALTAR
Secrets of the Kalyva Crown
by Lorraine Hall

King Diamandis finds solace in hard facts and duty. So, after a reckless night of abandon results in two heirs, marriage is nonnegotiable! The challenge is convincing his former assistant, Katerina Floros, to see that too...

#4119 HER DIAMOND DEAL WITH THE CEO
by Louise Fuller

When lifeguard Ondine rescues Jack Walcott from drowning, she almost regrets it. The billionaire is as rude and entitled as he is gorgeous, so Ondine doesn't expect any thanks. And certainly not his convenient marriage proposal!

#4120 ONE NIGHT IN MY RIVAL'S BED
by Melanie Milburne

Grayson Barlowe's always been my enemy, yet I've never been immune to his devilish good looks. We were taught to compete on the business battlefield. Now, working together requires a truce that has landed me in the place I vowed I'd never be—*between his sheets!*

HPCNMRB0523

HARLEQUIN
PLUS

Try the best multimedia subscription service for romance readers like you!

Read, Watch and Play.

Experience the easiest way to get the romance content you crave.

Start your **FREE TRIAL** at
www.harlequinplus.com/freetrial.